STATION OF DEAD HEARTS

Station of Dead Hearts
by Falguni Ephji
Paperback Edition

First Published in 2024 in India by

Inkfeathers Publishing
Vivek Vihar, New Delhi 110095
www.inkfeathers.com

Content Curation Partner

ISBN 978-81-19483-75-4

STATION OF DEAD HEARTS

A New Hope

FALGUNI EPHJI

INKFEATHERS PUBLISHING
www.inkfeathers.com

CONTENT CURATION PARTNER

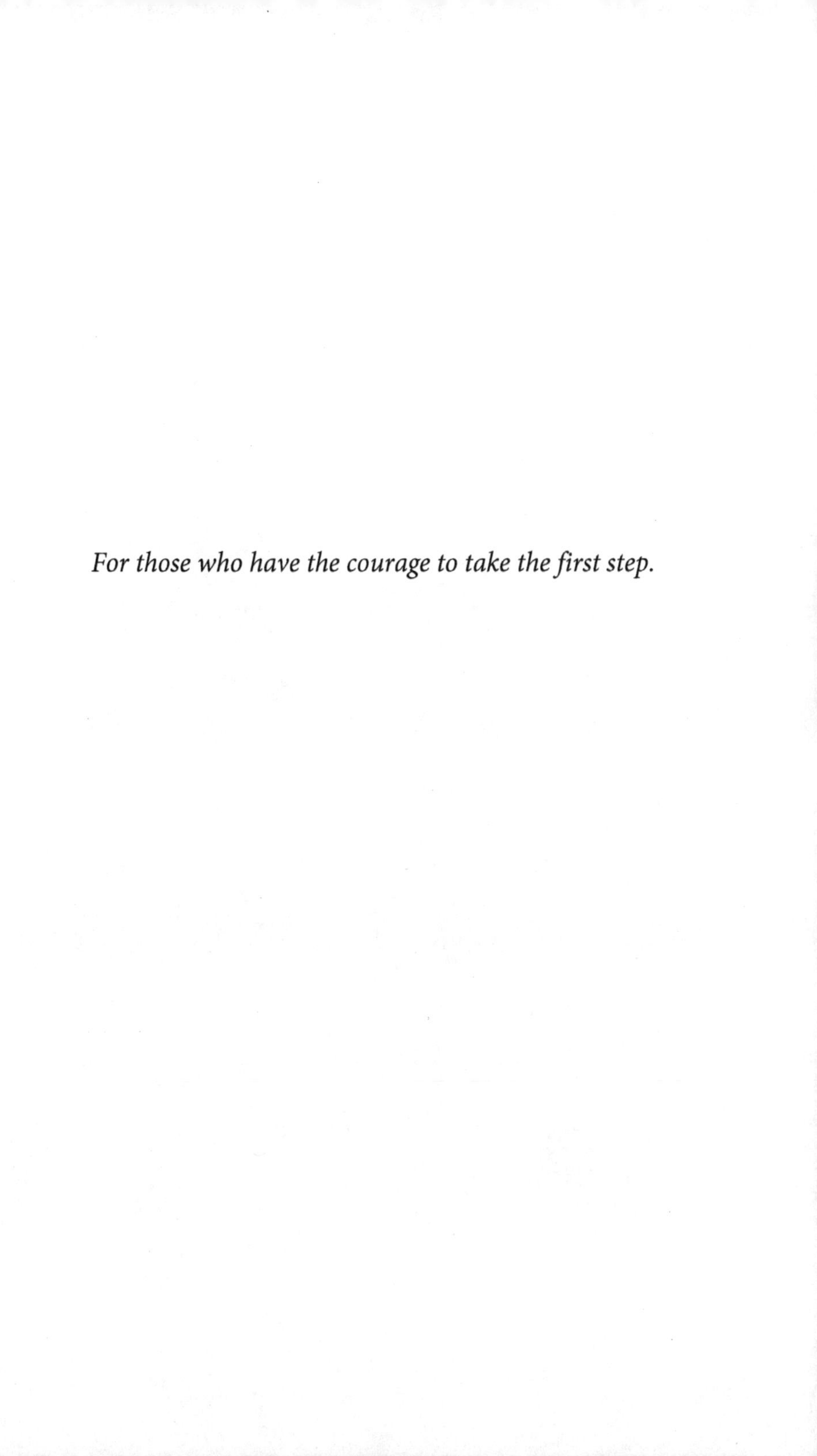

For those who have the courage to take the first step.

I believe many of you have heard that

'KARMA ALWAYS RETURNS,'

but do any of you know how?

Then gear up; I'm taking you on a deep ride of

it.

Contents

1.

To The Unknown

It can't be! No, please help! You can't just let them die! So much blood! Oh my God! What should I do? Are you even listening to me? Is anyone there to help? Please! Please listen to me! They're going to die! Please! No! It can't happen! What should I do? Hey! Hey, are you alive? Can you see me? Please! Please don't just die! Hey there! Please! Help us! Stop! Please! No, don't go! *(Panting repeatedly)* Whoa! Was that a dream? Was I just dreaming? That was so real! Such a horror it was! I still have Goosebumps! But, why am I feeling like this? My throat! I can't... I... *(coughing)* can't breathe! Why am I not able to breathe properly? And what's wrong with my eyes? Why is it all black? Did I go blind somehow? It's not comfortable at all! And the place... Yes, the place! Where am I? I can't even move my body. It's way too stiff. My hands are getting numb! Cold! Cold! It's cold right there! My legs are all curled! I can't feel my body anymore! There's unbelievable stiffness… as if I have turned into a complete rock! What's wrong with all my bones? And the joints! Are they not working? Am I going to die? or... have I already passed that stage? Is this the feeling of after death? Is death this much painful? No! No, it can't be! What's wrong with me? Why am I thinking about all these mortal things? I have to get out of here! It's hard! The place is too small to move. I'm pushing, but it seems like... I'm trapped! Am I locked in this place? But why? What did I do? I can't remember anything! But it's too painful in there! I want to get out of here. I have to try again. I have to try to be free. *(struggling noise)* Oh! Finally! It's open, and I'm going to get out of there. I struggled and somehow managed to get out of the place, but while standing up, my head made contact with a solid object, and trust me, it aches! While standing in a proper way, I realised a sudden sensation all over my body, and all my bones were making a weird, peculiar noise, as if they had been in a deep, undisturbed slumber for an extended period of no activity. Currently, my hands are the only support for my back. I wish I could have a stick or something to hold right now. After several tries, I am now able to move my body, and to assess the condition of my legs, I am conducting a brief trial walk. *(breathing softly)* Ah! Fresh air! To realise that I can now smell freedom with no pain brings a smile to my face. I am now trying to enjoy my freedom and feel all my body, which was almost numb some minutes ago. Some time passed, and I got back to the realisation that not only my body but also my eyes are now in very good condition, and they can see almost everything, and now I can appreciate how beautiful the... My words could not turn into a sentence as soon as I realised where I was right now. Everything is some sort of... Some sort of... I can't describe the oddness of this place. Everything is white in colour right there. If I am not very wrong, it is a station, a train station most probably, but I have zero idea from what point of view this station has nothing—typically nothing! My confusion and curiosity reach their peak as soon as I turn my face to the backside. It is a bench, a large white bench, which is standing all alone on this wide station. The colour is merging with the entire station, but what is more surprising is the fact that the bench is not making any shadow. It is quite weird! Is it not? I have never seen something like this before! While scrutinising from maximum to minimum details, my eyes are drawn to the underside of the bench. It is black! It is completely dark under there, and that darkness is somehow giving me terror. If the bench is not making any shadows, then why is the area under the bench dark? It looks like someone painted it a black colour! Something is wrong with the place down there. It is terrifying to me… As if something is gawking at me with an unusual threat! That's sending shivers down my spine, and I can almost feel the beads of sweat tracing a chilling path along my back. With a hesitant gulp, I decide to delve deeper into the secret behind the darkness.

But as soon as I bend, I see nothing down there, which is surprising. But the more surprising it becomes when I realise that some time ago I, myself, was lying down there! Yes, I am probably sure about that! Because the station has nothing but this white bench! But how did I end up in this place? What happened to me? I was so lost in my thoughts when suddenly, a bright flash of light forced my eyes to shut, leaving me numb. The light is so harsh that I cannot open my eyes. It's like my hands are the only support to help me in this condition! It takes some moments for me to adapt to what just happened. I gently remove my hands to let my eyes see what the matter is. There is a train slowly approaching the platform. The train, painted in a deep, foreboding black hue, is moving forward ominously towards the platform, evoking an aura of mystery and tension. All of a sudden, I frowned my eyebrows intensely, casting a shadow over my expression. The piercing blast of the whistle echoed through the ear. It blows my mind and shakes me with the realisation that the train has stopped right in front of me. The gateway of the train is right in front of me, which has a darker vibe than the train itself. If I describe the entire scene right in front of me in a quite simple way, then it is like a train that is black in colour with a gateway that is much darker, as if someone added some extra layers of black while painting the train's gateway itself. The train's gateway exuded an unsettling and suspicious energy, as if concealing secrets within its depth. Peering through the other side, I can see a picture that is somehow not sharing a clear image. I am sure there is an image of a person who is looking at me. Is it just an image? or... it is a person itself? Actually, to be honest, I was scared some time ago because of these surroundings and the uncanny things happening, but now, I am getting numb! The image in the picture is moving! My heart is racing uncontrollably; I can hear that! And also, the audible sound of my own nervous gulp echoed in my ears. Beads of sweat formed on my forehead. I am all cold right now, and I don't know what to say or what to do! But... But the image on the other side is attracting all the attention insanely! As my skin is all covered with sweat, I raise my hands to wipe it off! But when I was doing that, my eyes became transfixed by the image before me. The image in the picture is moving synchronously with my actions! My eyes are all wide right now! I am breathing heavily! The image is looking right at me, too! Our eyes lock, and the face is gawking at me with the same emotion as if it were reflecting myself. The nervous me is looking here and there to find out if anyone else is present or not, but surprisingly, there is no one. I suddenly feel alone, with the only reflection left on this huge platform! The image is terrifying, with all the bruises all over the body. The skin complexion is paler and more translucent, which does not seem real, and the white dress that the image is wearing is all shattered. The crimson hue has spread creepily over the dress. I was observing every single detail of the image, and all of a sudden, I had the thought to have a quick look at myself. So, I look down, and what I see is a white dress, the same as shown in the picture, but it has no marks! I thought to check my face to see if it aches because of any bruises, but no, it is also clear! There is nothing on my face, but the image does. The more I am trying to find a connection, the more it becomes clear that it's me in the mirror, but from another time and another life. I am standing in front of the entrance of the mysterious train and thinking about all the incidents. All of a sudden, a chilling voice, laden with suspicion, whispered hauntingly into my ear, sending shivers down my spine. The voice is not clear, so it is difficult for me to understand what it is exactly trying to say, so I decide to take a sharp ear to the whispers. I stand still until I feel like the unclear voice is trying to lead me into the train. The more I listen to it, the more I am losing control over my true self. I can feel that something is fishy here! The dark, mysterious secret of the train is driving me to the brink of insanity! It is somehow casting a chaotic spell on my senses to pull me into the UNKNOWN.

2.

Recognition of Beatrix

I should not go there. Or should I? Why is everything so hazy? Why can't I focus on my inner self? It is like someone, or something is slowly possessing me! My eyes are losing their focus. All I can see is the darkness of this train, as if I am about to be lost in this wide darkness. It will eat me! I... I should not go... I could not complete my sentence as a sudden thunderous blast shattered the silence and stopped all the chaos at the same time as the haunting wail of the train whistle pierced through the air, sending shivers down my spine, and jolting me into a state of sudden awareness. I was left breathless, gripped by an overwhelming surge of fear and surprise. As a result, I stepped inside the train all of a sudden. I was so startled that I did not realise that I would be trapped in such a situation that the doorway got locked as soon as I stepped inside. It is more like I am forced to do something out of my own wish. Stepping into the dimly lit train coach, an unsettling wave of uncertainty washes over me. The beating sound of my own heart is going wild. The darkness obscures my surroundings, leaving me with an unsettling sense of the unknown. I can't see anything, but for sure, I can sense the foul! Something is not normal in there! There is a disgusting odour that is lingering in the air, which is adding a layer of discomfort within me. That darkness is whispering secrets and heightening the tension in the air. I can sense that my entire body is getting numb because of an unsettling sensation. The gate of the train is locked, but ironically, the train itself is still not moving. I was the only passenger on the entire platform, and if I am right here inside the train, then why has the train not started yet? What is the reason behind its stiffness? I could not think anymore as I suddenly got a flashback of myself stuck beneath the bench some time ago. Is it an illusion? Am I still dreaming? What is wrong with me today? It's too much confusing!

'Hey.' *(humming noise)* 'Hey there.' And that's when I felt like my soul would leave my body at any time. I slowly turned my sight to my right, and what I saw was unforgettable. There was nothing but a black layer of shadow, which is way darker than the train itself. The atmosphere of this train coach is somehow giving me a negative vibe, and the vibe is strong enough to make me go sick. I am so stunned right now that, sometimes ago, I was thinking I was the only one who was present in this train or in this trap, but no, no, I am not alone here! Though I can't see anyone in front of me, I can feel the terror that is coming from the view there. It is like some stars in a broad sky; they are staring at me. From this moment on, I can tell that I am going to have some crazy encounters so far. The eyes are sparkling like an animal, and all their gaze is focused on me, giving me a living terror. But why are they not moving? I am also looking at them with amazement; the same sense of curiosity and fear is working on me. That's why my eyes are all focused on them without any movement. But what is their reason? Why are they not blinking? Are they also surprised after seeing someone here? Did they all go through the same states as me while entering this coach? Did they all get trapped? Are they going to understand my situation? No, no! What am I thinking? There must be another reason for all of these things! I should embrace only the positive among all the negatives. I am trying to soothe the racing beats of my heart, calming the frantic palpitations, but I can't focus on myself anymore as the continuous sound of whispering is distracting me. The darkness is calling me; it has enveloped everything, swallowing even the faintest glimmers of hope within me. I am standing frozen, confused by the indescribable feeling within me. I know there is no other way open for me; I know I am all covered in fear of the unknown right now, but still, I have to do something. Standing here, scrutinising all the details of the coach, and praising the depths of darkness, is not going to be the solution for me. I have to make a move, so I chose to navigate the darkness. Heart racing, palms slick with sweat, I mustered courage and stepped forward, and I walked into the seemingly insatiable mouth of darkness. I am walking slowly with all my senses left open. I am breathing repeatedly and soundlessly, as I don't want to make any noise. I know all eyes are focusing on me; without my consciousness, they are watching and monitoring my every step. I know I will be caught by all, but still, I don't want to make myself go in public; maybe I am not ready to face them. The blackness of the place is making the air feel heavy and suffocating, which is somehow leaving me with an unsettling sense of solitude. The more I move forward, the more my sight turns hazy. My legs are trembling, and I have no idea where I am going to end up. I am slowly doubting my own decision to be brave and have decided to stay. My breath is getting heavier, and my heart starts to beat faster. To be honest, I am expecting something mysterious, and I know this is going to panic me. With cautious steps, I am about to cross the threshold. I am now at the climax of the situation. I am slowly squeezing my eyes out of fear. One step, two steps, and the last step is going to reveal all the secrets. Immediately after reaching that spot, my left eye widened, and I started to lose control over my body! The irony of the situation struck me like a lightning bolt. Sometimes ago I was preparing myself for the unknown; I was ready to face everything, but... but this twist makes me speechless. There is no one in my sight. The compartment is empty, devoid of any life! A chill crawled up my spine as a sense of unease settled deep within my bones and my limbs. I can see there is no one, but still, I can't get rid of an uncertain fear. Why? Why am I feeling like I am not alone? But the place is completely empty; it is clearly visible. Then... why am I having the feeling that I am still being watched by someone? What's wrong here? Something is undeniably wrong in this place. The desolation and the oppressive darkness are creating a confusing atmosphere for me. I am shaking, my legs are getting tired, and they can't hold me any longer! I took a gulp and looked here and there, but I couldn't find anyone to help me with that situation right now. The high tension that has been created within me is causing a sort of issue with my breathing and my energy. No, no, I can't stand it anymore! There is no one, but at the same time, I feel like I am in the custody of many people! What is this feeling? This is so new for me! I have not faced anything like this in my entire lifetime. Like my inner self, my eyes are also numb; they refused to accompany me in this situation. I am too afraid to keep looking at this awkwardness! Now I need to calm myself down! I need to take a rest! Every fibre of my being cried out for respite. At that moment, I saw there was an empty seat near the window, which enlightened my hope and gifted me a wide smile of relief on my face. It was really hard for me to even walk to that seat on my own, but still, with sheer determination, I pushed through the fatigue and struggled towards the seat. With great relief, I eased myself into the seat, sinking into its warm embrace.

Aahh!! Finally! It's a relief!

I close my eyes and try to feel the comfort of this moment by forgetting all that happened earlier. But suddenly, I noticed a faint glimmer of light illuminating my seat amidst the encompassing darkness. It's not like the light is coming from the platform; hardly any light is coming from the window! It is more like I am now in the spotlight; it's now easier to scrutinise every detail of mine. Why am

I only thinking about negativity today? What is exactly wrong with me? I am trying to convince myself to behave normally in this case, but... but my senses are telling me something different! I can hardly receive any approval from my inner self to sit in peace. My overthinking got interrupted as I was jerked by a sudden force that almost pushed me backward, though it took me some time to maintain. I am sitting right now, but I am still balancing and adjusting to the changing motion. I am grabbing my seat tightly and taking the initiative to look at my right side. By looking at the outside view of the window, I realise that the train starts to move slowly. There is a mix of emotions enveloping me. I can't understand if I should be happy or not! I have left that weird station and those unpredictable moments, but what about the compartment itself? I am still in there! The darkness of this compartment speaks much fouler than the platform! The oppressive darkness cloaked every inch of this compartment. It seems as though I am imprisoned within a cage of ominous events. Each moment is pregnant with the potential for danger! The rhythmic chugging and swaying of the train echoed through the dense atmosphere, making me feel the loneliness; it was like amplifying the unease that settled within me. Just when the plaguing thoughts began to gnaw at the edges of my psyche, a sudden interruption cleaved through my musings. Unexpectedly, a hand materialised in front of me. It is more likely to be popped up from nowhere and holding a piece of food; it said, 'Take this.' The sight of it juxtaposed against my trepidation offered me a sliver of comfort—a human touch in the uncanny void. It was like my senses got back to their natural rhythm! The voice was that of a lady with a gentle ambience, offering me a piece of snack. I immediately look upward with a wide smile to welcome my fellow passenger. I was curious and confused at the same time, and I followed the hand with my gaze to catch a glimpse of this kind stranger. But instead of the comforting sight of a human face, I was greeted with a blank voice! With open jaws and incredibly surprised eyes, I kept looking at the blank view... What is this? What is this thing? I can't see any face, as if the dark had eaten its head and the body. But the hands, as if they were hanging independently, sprouting from the abyss, not attached to any human form. A cold drop slides down my head, and the comforting warmth that had embraced me some time ago is fading dramatically. I thought I finally got company, and I was not alone in this uncanny journey, but I was wrong! I am wrong! I am all alone once again. There is no one who can understand my feelings right now or what I am going through right now. Nobody is going to understand me here. My whole body is getting cold once again; there is no more warmth of any kind. My thoughts couldn't end up in imagery as it's cut by a sudden female voice: 'Here it is! Keep this with you. You will not get food for a long time. You...' I didn't let her finish and threw a question: 'Wha...what? No, thank you! Who are you? I am okay. I don't need any food.' 'There will not be any stoppage, so keep this with you, girl.' The words left me in deep thought. Why no stoppage? What does that even mean? And why is she speaking like this? She is helping me with food. She is offering me her share; if she might be a kind soul, then why does her voice sound like this? The voice has no emotion! What is the reason behind that? 'Wh...Wha... Why will there not be any stoppage? And why are you talking to me from such a distance? Ca... can't you come? I mean, don't you think talking to each other by facing each other would be an excellent choice?' I asked out of huge curiosity, and it also took me a good amount of courage to ask her to come and unfold her secrecy. I am taking deep breaths after talking to her like that! Anyone can guess by my behaviour that I am nervous right now. I waited for a reply that would comfort my palpitations, but there has been no reply so far. But her hand is still there, in the gesture of offering me food. It took me some time to realise that what I was looking at was not the hand of a human. I mean, how can someone's skin look like this? There is something wrong with her hand! Her skin is shining, and it's not normal. There is probably a layer of something concrete over her skin. The amount of curiosity raised in me was enough that I couldn't hold myself back from taking the initiative to touch her hand. As soon as I raise my hand to touch, that hand started moving backward. I felt quite ashamed and moved my hand back quickly!

"I am sorry! I didn't mean to make you uncomfortable. I was simply curious."

"Curious about what?"

The gloomy voice of the woman turns into a rough one. That voice was horrible enough to make me terrified. So I decided to make things clear.

"Hey, I'm asking your pardon for what I said earlier. That was a misunderstanding! I don't want you to go mad at me just for a misunderstanding. We are the only ones right here. So we should behave like friends, right? We are friends, right?"

I took a pause after finishing my sentence. There was no reply from the owner of that hand. But after some time, the hand that was my only hope in this uncanny place, now left me startled. There is an awkward, pin-drop silence that is making me uncomfortable.

Ah! I just messed up! I should not have asked this kind of question anymore. She tried to help me, and I messed up with her with bad behaviour. I should clarify my words!

"Hey there, I am really sorry! You don't need to hide yourself! You can be comfortable with me. We are after all each other's fellow passengers. We are friends on this journey, right? Are... are we not friends?"

"We are not friends."

A sharp and cracked male voice answers my question in a very practical way! I left shocked! "I thought we were just two in there, but you... I am. I mean. Nice to meet you, sir. But where are you? I can't see you either." I am asking after having huge courage and curiosity, but I am not going to ask anything that will hurt anyone's emotions. Simultaneously, I am trying to hide my own condition right now. I don't want to let them know that I am totally down in fear, though my voice and continuous sweats are clearly saying something else. I don't know how long I will be able to continue this pretending game. But I know somehow things will be mysterious to me!

I was about to say something to them, then all of a sudden, I got startled by a group of husky voices slowly repeating the same phrase.

"The train will not stop anymore."

"This train will not stop."

"Yes, yes, the train will not stop anymore."

I was surprised after hearing all these words from those unpredictable voices echoing through the air. Each rendition of the words sent shivers down my spine, stirring a furious blend of terror and apprehension within me. I found myself engaged in a heart-and-mind battle over whether to say something or to stay silent. I was stuck in this tormenting dilemma, and then within a minute, a pair of indistinct eyes flickered through the enveloping darkness, freezing me in my tracks. The sight sent an icy jolt of fear coursing through my veins, rendering me momentarily paralyzed. All eyes are gazing at me with an unknown, emotionless gesture. The atmosphere is covered with such uncertain silence that the sound of my gulp echoes through the air. I don't know what to do. I am feeling completely weird right now. After some time, I became aware of a distant murmur.

"Who are you?"

Another voice said,

"What's your name?"

Another male voice asked,

"Where did you come from?"

"Who are you?"

The same repeating question is simple and innocent enough in its essence, but it is also powerful enough to make me struggle to think again. Who am I, and where did I come from? What is my name? Who am I? My whole existence seems like a question mark to me. I don't know who I am. How can't I remember anything? What is my identity?

"What happened? Who are you?"

I was so lost in my thoughts that I almost forgot where I was. It was like an incomplete dream, thinking about my identity. I clear my throat and am about to answer their questions. But as soon as I started speaking, I had nothing to say except repeat their own question again and again. "Who am I? Umm, who am... I am... I am... my name, my name is... My name is." Suddenly, a man with a harsh and rude voice interrupted me by saying,

"Come on! Speak the truth! Who are you? You are one of those nasty brats, right? You can only ask for it! I'm not going to share anything with you, you poor beggar! You... you..."

By cutting his words, I replied, "I am Beatrix. My name is Beatrix."

After saying that, a realisation jerked me back to reality. What have I just said? What was that? I can hardly remember anything about my identity; then why did I speak that name? Without my own concern, I just told them my name is Beatrix. It is more like someone else said that instead of me. There is something I can't remember, but it is still happening within me. Who is Beatrix? Why did I address myself as Beatrix? What on earth is happening with me?

3.

Mystery Begins

I was all lost in my own thoughts, rectifying the continuous tug of war between my mind and my heart. But I didn't miss the chance of noticing the fact that all the eyes, which were shining in the darkness, have now vanished and are no longer visible. My senses are still alert, as they can feel that someone is looking at me. I thought I should talk to them. I guess they will not harm me. They were trying to offer me food. It is an act of kindness! They must be good people! Then why don't they come in front of me? Why are they talking from a distance? Are they thinking I am going to harm them? No way! Then it is a misunderstanding! I am not going to harm them! And why would I? Did I behave badly towards them? Everyone would behave like me if they were at my state! Everything is weird right here! From the very beginning, I have been facing difficult situations. Everything has been new to me. It's my normal reaction to all these new but uncanny things. I did not behave rudely towards them. I... Then... yes, yes, the food! They gave me it out of care and empathy! I think I should have taken this. Can I ask for it now? Will they mind giving that to me again? Okay, let's give it a try! I should ask them now. Um, excuse me, can I get the food that you were going to give me at that time? What was that? A cookie, yes! That cookie! I really would love to have that. I was facing the deep depths of darkness when I saw a hand slowly coming in front of me from the black background. That hand... the lady... "Oh! Yes! The cookie! So kind of you. Thank y..." My words couldn't get to the end, as I had a clear observance of that hand. What on earth is this? When I first saw that, I thought her skin was shining and glowing like gold, but no. It is... it... it is gold itself! Numerous gold coins covered her skin and her metal-like hand—is it a costume or what? I thought I should ask her about her hand. I could not. I couldn't sound so mean at my first meeting. By simply ignoring the view of her hand, I move my right hand forward to take the food. I look down and try to maintain a simple face. I was about to take the food when my eyes get stuck to her nails. Wha... what is this? Is it blood? Her nails are all broken and painted with blue spots as if a blood clot, and her nail tips are filled with a crimson hue as if blood. Her nails are making me think about what happened to her. I think she might have harmed her hand while travelling; after all, the place is completely eclipsed by shadow and darkness. It is hardly possible to look at anything in the surroundings. She must be hurt. I shifted my thoughts from her nails to the food, and I was about to touch the food when I felt that something inside me was stopping me from taking that cookie, but I rather chose not to create any scene, and finally, I took that cookie. Now it is in my hand. I am holding it, and I'm about to sniff it, as it is my natural behaviour to sniff before eating anything. I believe cooking is a very beautiful art that must be praised with all our senses. I was about to lift that cookie upward and smell it, but then suddenly I saw something moving. Something was moving on the cookie. I thought I was seeing wrong because of the darkness and was about to put that inside my mouth, but then I myself stopped me to give it a detailed examination!

As soon as I started scrutinising the cookie with a sharp eye, I was left speechless. The food is not edible! All the food is covered with bacteria, parasites, and other disgusting things. I divide the cookie to have a look, and the truth leaves me startled as I can clearly see that the food is totally made with fungi, parasites, and many more poisonous toxins. It's not food at all. It's gross! Completely gross! They tried to feed me this shit. How dare they! Almost bursting out of anger, I looked upwards and took the initiative to talk to them about this bad behaviour and let them answer me about why they did that to me! I could not move any further on my initiative, as I was stunned to see she was offering me that cookie once again! I don't need this shit, thought I, and aloud I said, 'No thank you, I don't need to eat right now. I am full!'

"Take this; you will need it after some time. There will not be any food. So keeping this will be a wise decision for you," the lady explained loudly. I was stunned! Can't they see I caught their motive red-handed? The gross is now clearly shown. Then why are they offering this again? I mean, what's wrong with their behaviour? Are they joking around with me? But her voice, the emotionless voice, and the way she is talking to me are saying something different! Is there something else behind their behaviour? Or is it normal for them? No! No! How can it be normal for someone to eat? Maybe she didn't do this on purpose. Maybe it's my bad luck to find only this gross cookie out of a hundred or many, probably!

I think I should ask for another one or... something else than this to eat! Yes, let's ask, "Umm... I mean... I actually don't want to offend you, but that cookie was a complete shi... umm... I mean... can I have something else? Plea.. please?"

"We have only this! We don't have anything else. Eat this! Eat this!"

"No, thank you! Thanks for your kindness!' but not this one. Thank you for offering me,' I replied with minimum genuineness! By that time, I glanced at her hand, as it had been bothering my eyes for a long time. So, out of curiosity and enthusiasm, I decided to touch her hand, but as soon as I raised my hand to touch her hand and as my fingertips made contact, an icy breeze enveloped my hand. Yet, to my disbelief, my fingers passed through it, leaving me with an unsettling sense of contact with the ethereal. As if... as if I just went through the boundaries between the living and the unseen. I can't describe my feelings right now. I am feeling cold right now; a sudden drop in temperature sends shivers down my spine. What just happened to me? My rising emotions are clearly visible on my face. I am now taking repeated breaths, my eyes are left in an extra-large shape, and my jaws are now dropped. What on earth is this? "Who are you?" I loudly asked after taking my hands back with a flinch of time. I was shocked by a sudden touch, but that touch not only had an effect on me but also caused chaos in that compartment. The lady whom I touched is now crying loudly, and everyone is shouting, talking to each other, and making weird noises. But mysteriously, all things are happening behind the unseen, as if darkness is trying to hide them continuously. In the chaos, one thing is all I can hear clearly. The name is Beatrix.

'She is here!'

'Hmm! Beatrix is there. She is Beatrix.'

'She is her.'

'Yes, yes, she is her.'

'It is that Beatrix.'

'She can do it; only she can do it.'

They are crying and repeating the same phrase again and again. They are talking about me! Me? I mean Beatrix! They are talking about Beatrix. But who is Beatrix? What did she even do? Then, am I caught? Do they somehow know that I even don't know who Beatrix is, but I am claiming that I am Beatrix?

But why even spell that name? What's the story behind this name? What am I going to do now? Is Beatrix good or bad? Did she do something wrong? Is she punishable? What am I going to say if they ask me? And by taking the name of the devil, the devil is here.

'Are you Beatrix? That Beatrix?' one of them asked me curiously.

I am hesitating because I don't know what to say. I thought it would be a better idea to nod my approval; at least by doing so, they would present their original selves to me, as it is clearly visible that they know Beatrix. After all, I am all alone in this uncomfortable, uncanny place with these weird people.

'Yes, yes, I am Beatrix, but... whm?

I was about to say why, but I could not finish my word as I was interrupted by a sudden noise. A couple of people are crying, whipping, and making creepy noises of pain and sorrow.

'We were waiting for you,' a male voice echoed in the compartment. 'Yes, yes, we were waiting,' others kept repeating the same lines.

'Why?' I asked with a gentle gesture.

'Wh... why were you waiting for me? What... what is wrong with you?'

The lady cried out loudly, stopped my words, and, for the first time, stepped out of the darkness. The more she is trying to come forward, the more my hands are getting numb, and my legs are becoming heavier to move. I am now leaning backward to stick to my seat. As she came into view, it was impossible not to be struck by the sheer magnitude of her presence. The lady is standing tall and imposing, her figure exuding an aura of robustness that seems to defy gravity itself. Like her body, her face is also well-rounded. Thick black hair frames her face, adding to the intensity of her appearance. From her mouth, a viscose red liquid trickle slowly. The thickness of the liquid and the marks on the dark red edges of her improper teeth signify that it is a juice of *paan* (an Indian mouth freshener made from betel leaf) that trickles slowly, leaving a trail of vibrant colour in its wake. She is wearing a red-layered white *saree* (an Indian traditional female attire). From her unsettled and unpinned *saree* and her messy hair, one can assume that she is not a well-arranged person. But what is most surprising is her skin. It is shimmering with an iridescent glow, looking more like a layer of concrete. It is glowing even in this dark hue. It made me start stuck, and I couldn't resist myself and asked her:

'What is this? What is there on your skin?'

The lady is not at all surprised. It is like there is no emotion left in her. Without any excitement, she raises her hand on the zero to let me see her body clearly. I cannot believe my own eyes anymore! What I just saw—am I dreaming, or what on earth are these things? How can it be even possible? I was thinking it was a mask of concrete or some stuff like that, but I never even thought it could be turned out like this. No way, the lady is covered with layers of coins. Coins of different shapes have overpowered her flesh. There is no skin left on her, instead of that, she has metallic coins all over her body! It can't be true! I must be dreaming! How can someone have all these things on their body? It is not at all human-like. I was surprised enough, but then suddenly the woman cried out loudly,

'We were waiting for you.'

'Come with us.'

'Us? How many of you are present right now?' I asked curiously.

'See for yourself.'

'Wh... what do you mean... what do you mean to see?'

'Here, this way, come with me; they are waiting for you.'

'Who is waiting for me? And why?'

'Come here,' and by that, the lady turned around and started moving backwards. Without any further questioning, I followed her. With a shaking leg, I stepped forward. The compartment is very dark, and it doesn't allow me to walk properly. The colour of this darkness is much darker than anything one can ever imagine! Despite all my problems walking properly because there is no light, I keep following the lady's introduction. The more I'm stepping into the coach, the more it gets bigger. It is no longer a regular train coach. The depth is spreading magically, as if it itself were a world. World of darkness. There is no light in any compartment, for sure, but things are now becoming visible one by one. The compartment is empty, but there is something like a suitcase situated right on the seat of one of the compartments. I could not focus more on the suitcase as the lady suddenly sat on the bench facing me. The view is terrible! She and her entire body are bouncing like jelly, and her coin-like skin is melting like heated concrete. How can it be possible? She is looking at me; her eyes are not in place, and her mouth, filled with the red juice of *paan* is getting bigger! She is bouncing and almost in a state to melt on the seat; her outfit is like denying covering her naked self, and it is sliding from her coin-like skin. I am getting goosebumps! What am I watching right now? I am dreaming, right? But why is it feeling so freaking real? My voice is getting numb, and my throat is turning into a rock out of disbelief and fear! She can't be real! The suitcase beside her now catches my gaze, and it leaves me in awe. The abundance of gold coins is now showering like a miracle from her suitcase, but somehow it is not bothering me, and now my only focus is on the lady, as she is calling me by her hand, which is melting continuously, giving me live terror.

'Beatrix.'

'Beatrix, come here.'

No, not a single time here. I thought, and aloud, I replied,

'I am dreaming, right? I need to wake up first.'

'No, it's all real! Now come to me, Beatrix!' She confirmed the situation and kept calling me.

Without further discussion, I decided to leave the place. As soon as I turned back, all I could see was the doorway to another compartment. I moved to that side. The dimness of that compartment is giving me another invitation to explore something unexpected. The more I am thinking, the more my heart is racing faster. Because of my fear of the unknown, I was about to stop there, but when I turned back, I saw the lady with a horrible figure coming towards me and all about to touch me. After watching that, without any delay,

I turn back and start running towards another compartment. The lady can see me emerging into the darkness. The more I am running, the more the place is getting bigger. Where is the exit? There is nothing to find. Is this place empty? Is no one here? Or only I can't see anything, and... and they can see me? I can't run anymore. *(Panting repeatedly)* I am tired. I need to stop. At that point in time, I found a window. I move forward to it to see the outer world, but... what is this? The same station? The train is moving, but why are the platform and everything in the station the same? The same white surface, everything is whitewashed, no one in the entire station, the same white bench with no shadow but black ground... but wait! It is something weird with the bench! It looks more like the black colour of the ground is moving upwards as if it is going to cover the white colour of the bench! The legs of the bench are now black, and the body is white. It is different from the previous bench. That bench was totally white in colour, and there is a trash bin beside the bench that is totally black in colour. The colour of the bench is more likely similar to the colour of the bench's legs and the ground surface of the bench. They are creating an artistic effect with the station itself. But why the view of that place is same? As the train is moving fast and forward, the view might be different! Yes, it should be! But why is it all the same? While thinking all of this, all of a sudden, my eyes stuck when I looked at my dress. My dress is not the same as before; it is just the same as the bench, with my dress turning black from beneath. As if it is going to eat the white colour of the dress, the black colour is spreading. I cannot believe my own eyes. What am I witnessing? What's on earth are all of these? If it is not a dream, then what? Why are all these unreal things happening to me? I was thinking all these things, and then suddenly I could feel that all my senses have become alert! I could feel that I was being watched by someone. By taking a quick gulp, I turn back to face the upcoming situation. There is no one, completely no one, but I can feel that someone is there, at the corner of my sight! I decided to move forward to know what was there! When, after a few more steps, I reached that corner, I saw someone was sitting there facing me backwards. Just like my previous encounter with the lady, the place is very dark, though it must be impossible for me to see anything, but maybe I have a supernatural power to see things among this much darkness.

'Hello, anyone there? Can you tell me where the exit of this train is? I mean of this compartment?'

I asked that mysterious person with the hope of getting help.

'Why?' to surprise me I got a question as an answer to my own question from a husky, cracked male voice.

'Ba...be... because I want to get out of the train immediately.'

'You can't go anywhere! We were waiting for you for a very long time.'

'Why can't I go anywhere? And… why were you waiting for mm?'

I couldn't finish my word as he turned back to me. What a horrible creature it is! I can feel a cold chill run down my spine. What the hell is this? The man is gawking at me with his big, pale eyes and no emotion left on his face. From his one ear, a wire is hanging. Tilt slightly, and what I see is unreal! It is the wire of an earphone, but it is not hanging! It is coming out from inside his head! He has only one ear, and another one is missing, and instead of it, there is the wire of the earphone, as if his one ear is brutally chopped and blood is coming restlessly from there. He must be in pain. By looking at him, I am all getting cold and can't help but think about how painful this could be. Why is the man not crying or weeping? Is he not in pain? Can't he feel the pain? What is this gloomy, emotionless expression? All the time, he is staring at me with no emotion. By this time, I noticed that his one leg was being chopped, in the same condition as his ear. My eyes are getting bigger out of surprise, and I couldn't help but ask him.

'Hey mister? Are you alright? I mean, I know you are not right, but I mean, I am incredibly sad for your condition. But what happened to you?'

'Beatrix,' all he said was just this name!

'Yeah, I am Beatrix; do you need something? Can I hel...' Without letting me finish my word, the man opened his mouth and left me frozen on my spot out of disbelief! I was thinking that everything is normal with this man and that he might have gone through an accident that made him end up like this! But no! I was wrong! His mouth is getting bigger slowly, and his tongue is not that of a regular living human. It is like a long rope divided into two straps. And where he is sitting, there is an abundance of many electrical gadgets, and for no reason, they are multiplying, and the number of gadgets is increasing like the shape of his mouth! I was surprised by the incident, but it did not bother me anymore as I saw his tongue was about to come near me. I need to go. He is not normal! It can't be a normal, regular situation! I need to leave as soon as possible! But when I turned back, I couldn't move any further. In front of me, there is something or someone sitting in a corner of another compartment, and from here, it is more like a blurry image of an animal or something like that. By frowning my eyebrows, I am now walking towards that suspicious thing. Is it an image? Or, again, is it going to be something uncanny? I don't know what I am going to encounter this time. But why are all things like this on this train? What is happening to me today?! Everything is like a dream. A bad dream, for sure! Am I in a different universe? Did I do time travel and come to the future? I am thinking about all these unpredictable things, and without my own realisation, I am now in the middle of a compartment. Another compartment? Why are all the compartments in this coach this big? It is like a completely different world within every compartment. But... but... where is that animal? I mean, that image? That led me here; now where is it? Was that an illusion or something?

'So, they are telling the truth. Beatrix is present on this train.'

I was shocked by the sudden voice and was about to turn back, but when I turned back, I was stunned!

'Aaaaa!' a bone-chilling scream escaped from my lips in a high-pitched tone, by closing my eyes with my hands! I can't stand this anymore! What a terrifying face! My blood turned into ice in my veins! In front of me, there is a visage of sheer horror! A face so unsettling that it sent shivers cascading down my spine! The person before me is a live horror! His entire body is covered with a thick and wild coat of fur, as if he had been born of the wildness itself! The sight is definitely disturbing, but what is more disturbing are the countless wounds that riddle his furry frame! His face is also like the previous ones, with no emotion left in him! There is a necklace shining around his neck, making a contrast with his entire self! He is looking at me with his big, crimson eyes, and he is repeatedly licking his wounds, as if he is an animal trying to ease his suffering by licking his pain! I am almost about to lose control over my senses and my body. What on earth is he? Is he an animal or a human turned into an animal? And... and his one leg! It is brutally chopped, as if it's the result of an accident. I look at his surroundings; there are numerous bones and meat spreading here and there, and there are plenty of dry food like biscuits, cakes, etc. It didn't surprise me that much, and my eyes went on that furry beast like human!

He called me 'Beatrix,' with an unclear and unstable voice, he stared at me.

'We were waiting for you.'

'Come here.'

'We were looking for you.'

By saying this, he was about to get up from his place and was about to come to me. At that moment, I escaped that place and kept running and once again I ended up in another compartment. This time I encounter a miserable old man who has a disorder of eating. He is eating repeatedly, with a gloomy, pale look on his face! His belly is on the way to explode really soon, but still, he is eating! His head is turning right to left and left to right as a refusal, but his hand seems to not give a damn about any refusal.

As if the man is eating without his own concern. The more he eats, the more his belly gets bigger. And in his surroundings, he is sitting around a huge bump of cooked rice. The more he eats those rice, the more the pile of rice gets bigger and larger in number. Because of his disorder, his eyes are running from tears, but there is no sign of sorrow or pain on his face. Like others, he is also calling the name 'Beatrix' again and again. I was so done with the repeated situation, so I left that place, and out of disgust, I walked towards the next compartment. But after reaching the next compartment, I was numb. A pregnant man—yes, a pregnant man with a huge baby bump! The bump is getting bigger with every passing second. The more surprising and terrifying fact is that the bump is all transparent, and through that, I can clearly see the inside view. The view is much more disturbing than one can ever imagine. There are plenty of babies floating here and there within that bump, and the number of babies are increasing simultaneously with the size of that bump. I cannot believe in my own eyes. What I just saw is far more than just a bad dream. I am about to throw things out. I am moving backward to take any chance to escape that place. I start running, but the more I am running, the more the compartment seems bigger than before. As if there is no tomorrow. I am all trapped by the dark mystery of this compartment. After some restless running, I finally found the gateway. Ohh! Finally!! I am now going to get out of here. Enough of this madness. I can't stand this anymore. Now, finally, I am going to get rid of this drama! By saying that, I was about to step my one leg out of the door, but I couldn't and had to step further. There is a teenage girl floating in the air, but her two hands are stuck with the edge of the door stand, as if her hand is formed from the doorknob!

'Beatrix, you are finally here. We were waiting for you.' the girl told me.

'I want to leave! This place is cursed! I am not going to tolerate any kind of nonsense anymore!'

'Nonsense? It is not nonsense. Go back to them; they are waiting for you; we are waiting for you.'

'No! Please! Move aside! I want to leave!' I announced my refusal in a high-pitched tone. 'There is no way for you to leave. You can't escape Beatrix. It is your destiny! Go back to them.'"

"'No, I am not going,' I firmly declined, but then...

'Look at me; look at my situation.' By following her words, I looked at her, and I was all stunned! Her half-body is smashed! It is like a thin layer of paper floating spontaneously in the air! She has only half of her body! The dreadful view was enough for me to be stunned, but at the time, with big, pale eyes and a gloomy, emotionless face, she looked at me, saying,

'Look at my situation. It is because of you, Beatrix! You are responsible for this; you are responsible for everyone's situation!'

'Why are you blaming me?' cutting her words, I protest her!

'What did I even do? Why are you making me responsible for

your suffering? What is my fault? Why can't I remember anything?

'You are acting like a fool! You are the one, Beatrix. You are responsible for everything.'

'Then tell me what I did,' I said quite harshly!

'You want to know? Then go back to them. Ask them what happened to them. You are the reason, Beatrix! They are the reason!'

'They?? Wait a minute, who are they? What are you talking about? Who are the reasons beside me?'

'The reason is back in the compartment. Go back to them! Go back there, Beatrix."

4.

Karma

I totally have zero clue about what the girl is saying, but her words are now making me curious! Why would I do such terrible things to anyone? Is it me or just the name Beatrix? And who are the other people to whom the girl is throwing the blame for everything? By the time I look outside the train, it is the same, white-painted station with the bench and black trash bin. The bench is now almost painted black, just like the colour of its beneath! As it seemed suspicious to me, I turned my face down to look at myself, and yes, it is as I expected! My dress is also on its way to being totally covered with the colour black, just the same as the colour of the bench. I was expecting this, so I am not surprised at all! But the main surprising fact is my skin. There are some dark scars all over my bare skin, and my skin tone is getting lighter, but somehow not in a healthy way! The condition of my entire body is giving me a similar vibe, but somehow... I can't recall what the exact memory is. For a good amount of time, I was struggling. I really can't decide what to do in this situation, but the curiosity bestowed by the girl is making me wish to stay and know what the exact matter is here. I know the place is pregnant with uncanny and unreal happenings, and I know it can be much more dangerous if I go back to them all again. I know I know everything, but if all their suffering is the result of something I did, then I must go and apologise to them. Maybe it's because of the name Beatrix; maybe it's not me, but still, I am now willing to know what the real matter is! After all, I myself am also the victim. I am the one who is facing unexpected, mysterious occasions one by one from the beginning of the day. So, I have to know the reason behind it. By doing so, I move forward and back into the compartment. I kept walking until my destination arrived! The place is not new to me, so it will not give me terror, and I am not going to be afraid this time. I thought that, but reality hit me when I finally arrived at my destination. What is this place? Where have I just come? Is it the same place, the same I was in before? It's totally a different world! It is more likely a 3D film, and I am now a part of it! I am now in a bus, running on a busy road. Everyone on the bus is very busy minding their own business! Everyone is talking about catching the next train, or one after that. Perhaps this bus is going to lead all those people to a train station! The bus is almost full, and I am now in the middle of them. I can see them, and from now on, every noise in this bus is audible for me clearly! There are some empty seats, so I think I should go and sit there. I was about to go and sit there when a teenage boy pushed me and went to that seat to sit, but his pushing didn't have any effect on me, even though for some moment I thought he was going through me! What just happened to me? No, no! Maybe I am thinking too much! That was just a simple push, and...and I couldn't finish my word as a girl came closer to have a ticket from the conductor and is now standing on me, literally on me! I yelled at her! But she didn't care about my existence! Nobody does so! As I'm invisible for them! At that moment, I realised I am not a part of it; I am just a viewer! I can see them, and I can hear them, but they cannot! So, I have to watch them as a viewer, and it would be better to stay a ghost and watch them. There are now many passengers on the bus, and most of them are sitting, and some of them are standing and waiting for their turn to sit! Those who are already seated, are sitting by maintaining the seating format and guidelines. Like old people are on the seat of old citizens, the labelled handicapped seats are nicely occupied by people like them, ladies are sitting on their particular seat, and the same goes with the gents. Each and every seat is occupied in a proper manner, except for one seat among the seats for the elderly! I, myself as a female, am now sitting on a seat in the ladies' row, but actually I am sitting on the lap of a middle-aged aunty without even her concern! I am sorry, Aunty! I wish she could hear me for real. After some time, the bus stopped on a bus stoppage, and there were complete chaos. Someone is trying to get down from the bus while another is trying to get up by pushing each other. Of course, they have no time! After all, they are very busy; the next train is the gateway to their bright life! If they don't catch that, their entire life will be over! Huh!! They must be in a rush, or, I suppose, acting like they are in a rush! When the bus started once again, all the people started searching for a seat. No seat is available, so as a result of that, some are trying to pre-reserve the seat for the already-seated passengers, and some of them end up standing. The one remaining seat, no one is paying any attention to that as if it were from old citizen criteria! As no one is fulfilling the criteria and as no one is old here, the seat remains empty! All of a sudden, a man rushes towards the seat to sit! It is a middle-aged man in a loose suit and a cap who, without anyone's permission, reserves the seat, though he is not at all fulfilling the criteria! Maybe his heart is old enough to sit right there. I am pretty disappointed in that man, so I keep following his every movement. The man was about to raise his hand to open his hat. I was watching him, then suddenly an aunty came to preserve my seat. No, aunty, please, I am busy! Aah! Fine! Keep the seat. By telling her that, I gave my seat to her, but ironically, the seat is still not empty because I was not sitting on it! I was sitting on the lap of the aunt, who is sitting on the seat! For no reason, I end up standing almost over Aunty Number Two's feet! So I sit back on Aunty Number One's lap! While all this was happening, I forgot what I was doing! I was observing the middle-aged man sitting on an old citizen's seat. I think I should keep doing that! By that, I turn my face to that man, and that man is now without a hat, but as he is facing the outside of the window, it is impossible for me to see his face. By that time, the bus had reached a new stoppage. Same chaotic atmosphere with the same behaviour of passengers. But in that chaos, I can hear a lady's voice making a loud noise and telling others to be careful with her.

'Please move aside! Please move a little bit! I am pregnant! Please move! Please move your hand! Hey, hey, be careful, please!'

The lady is pregnant and has two heavy bags in her hands. She is trying her best to be careful with her baby bump! But no one seems concerned about her situation, which disappoints me. I was about to get up from Aunt's lap and take the bags from her hand, but my hands went through her. Okay! I am not visible here! I am sorry! I can't help you this time, sister! As the bags are heavy and the lady is stressed enough in this chaos, she is searching for a seat. But no one is willing to give her their seat, so she ends up standing among all the chaos! I can see she is scrutinising everywhere for a seat. Her face is stressed, and there are some beads of sweat slowly coming down her face. Maybe she is not feeling well! Then I saw her face and went towards the one seat on which the middle-aged man was sitting illegally. Her eyes are now shining with hope. With her two heavy bags, she is now leading towards the seat. I am now also happy, as finally the lady is going to have a seat. After all, she deserves that seat more than that weird middle-aged man.

'Excuse me! Can I have this seat?' the lady asked gently to that man. But the man seems unbothered by that question and is still looking outside the window. 'Umm, excuse me, please! This seat is for old citizens, and you are not like that, so please consider giving me the seat.' By breaking the silence, the man replies to her without facing her. 'I am not like, what?' being confused by his sudden behaviour, the lady answers after some moments. 'I mean, sir, you are pretty young, so I told you that! Please don't mind my words! I didn't want to offend you! I just wanted to say…'

'Then are you old?' Without letting her finish, the man threw another question. 'No! Sir! I am...' 'If you are not old, then why are you bothering me?' 'I am pregnant, sir.' The lady has now raised her voice a little bit higher than before, and that is totally right, though! Without knowing, without even glancing, how could he talk to her like that? He is a totally disgusting, uncultured person. But his voice! There is something wrong with his voice! Do I know someone who has the same type of voice? Or it is just a misunderstanding! By interrupting my self-talking, the man faces the lady, and the sight left me speechless. What the heck! And I was thinking, why is the voice too well known to me? Not only the voice, but the entire man is goddamn known to me! What the hell is going on? Where is his bump? Why is he all normal right here? That preg.... I could not finish my words, and my words were left incomplete as the man forced that lady behind all of a sudden! 'If you are pregnant, then what the hell are you doing here? Go and lock yourself in your home! Go and isolate yourself, you nasty bitch!'

The lady is now all stunned by this sudden rude behaviour, but she couldn't protest him and could only say, 'What did you say? I am like your sister's age; how could you say that to me?' The man gets up and raises her hand, and by making the gesture of slapping the lady, he says, 'So what? I said what was true! How dare you talk to me in such a high tone? Fuck off, you nasty bitch!' How dare that fucking bastard! You are the one who is nasty. You idiot! You bastard! You pregnant beast! I was so surprised by the man's behaviour and am continuously cursing that man. But what is more surprising is that none of the passengers on the bus resisted that fucking bastard! No one raised their voice against this offensive behaviour! Not a single person!! There are many males; no one resisted that incident. There are many females; no one supported that lady. The freaking beast is maybe uncultured; what he did was horrible and not human-like behaviour! Then what happened to all the other passengers? Are they also illiterate? Are they also horrible? Are they also inhuman? This is completely ridiculous! All the time, I couldn't pay attention to that lady, who is now a crying mess! By putting her head down, she is now crying without making any noise! Maybe because she is weeping without any pause, she is facing breathing problems. It seems like she can't catch her breath. The more I take the initiative to touch her and help her, the more I regret being invisible! The lady is now coughing but still somehow manages to hold her two bags tightly, as if it means a lot more than her entire life to her. She is coughing repeatedly! Everyone was looking, but no one! Literally, no one came forward to offer water! And all of a sudden, the lady collapsed in front of everyone and kept shaking in pain! That created a chaotic situation among the passengers. Her bags fell with her, and as she lost her grip, the bag opened up, revealing all that was inside! Sweater, little pair of socks, baby food, many toys, wool, and needles—all the things are now clearly visible, which is most probably for her upcoming baby. The crowd is moving here and there, leaving all the baby's things smashed on the ground! One of the aunts came to that lady to check, and within a minute, she nodded her refusal. The lady is no more! I have lost my hope. I have lost my speech. The lady is dead! The lady is now freaking dead!! She was going to be a mother. She, including her baby and her dreams to raise the baby, are now all dead! My eyes are now showering out of disbelief and sorrow! If anyone among the passengers would have come forward, if anyone of them would have helped her, if anyone of them would have offered her water, she could be alive! The baby could be alive! The dream could be alive! Because of the unbearable pain of insult, the pain of crying continuously, the pain of not being able to breathe, and the pain of not getting proper care and attention, she lost her life in a sudden heart attack. Because of that fucking bastard, she lost her life! She lost her baby, and... and that bastard is still looking outside without even looking at the dead body of that lady! With furious excitement, I got up from Aunt's lap and was about to hit the bastard, but suddenly, without any information, everything disappeared! Just disappeared! Everything is black once again! I am back in the darkness; the darkness of the gloomy compartment has gripped me once again. But the fear in me is no longer there! A ray of curiosity is all that I have now! I want to know the next story. I now understand what just happened to me. The story is here; now is my chance to read every page of this book! The more I am thinking about the pregnant bastard, the more I am getting furious and curious at the same time. I want to know the rest of their story too; I thought as I started walking towards the next compartment to unleash the next tale. As soon as I stepped into the next compartment, I found myself in a completely new world. At present, I am in the middle of a platform—a train platform—but not like the one I was on in real life today. It is a crowded, colourful platform, the imagery of which is perfect to be framed by an artist. There are some food stalls, there are some bookshops, and there's a ticket counter. Everyone is very busy once again. Of course, they have to catch the next train of their lives! But surprising enough, there are not only humans but also some cute furry babies—stray dogs and cats—roaming here and there. Some are following each other, some are following human beings, some are peacefully sleeping but with their bodies making a donut shape and hiding their tails as much as possible, and some are eagerly looking at the platform. Every one of them is doing different activities, but their basic needs for doing all those activities are the same: love, some food, and safety.

Suddenly, my eyes got stuck on a young puppy, patiently looking somewhere with a happy face and shining eyes that made me smile on my tired face. To check that place, I looked in the same direction where the puppy was looking. It is probably the most crowded place on the entire platform. It is a food stall, probably famous among the citizens! People are standing in long lines to make an order for their food. 'Make a single line! Hey, you, line up yourself! Make it a single line! Maintain the line! I repeat, make a single line!' And it continues. It's a male voice coming from inside the shop; most probably the shopkeeper is instructing the buyers to make a line. Whatever! I turn my face from that side; I better notice these cute little buddies. By then, I had moved forward to have a closer look at the little buddy outside the food stall. The moment my hands were about to touch the puppy to pet, it went through the puppy's belly! Ahh!! I am just a viewer! That's so mean! I wish I could feel this moment. At least this moment! This puppy is so cute! I observe every detail of that puppy and come to the conclusion that it is an indie male pup—the sweetest and bravest among all. I wish I could hug him and give him lots of good pets, but sadly, I can't. So, I sit beside him, of course, without his permission because he can't see me, and start observing his every movement. I noticed for a long time that, he has been staring at some sweets and bread. He must be hungry, but I need to appreciate that he is a very gentle dog! Despite being hungry and in front of a food stall at the same time, he has not done anything wrong yet! There is a waste bin where people are throwing away the waste of their ordered food. A man standing next to it is guarding that bin. Many dogs tried to eat some wasted food from there and ended up being chased in anger by that guard. But this puppy did not follow those other dogs! I am getting emotional by looking at them; their skeleton-like figure is making me sick! What will they do with that wasted food? Will they recycle that? Are they going to make art out of that wasted food? Then why are they making a fuss about this simple thing? I felt disappointed! Time has passed, and everything on the platform has not changed. A couple of trains came and went, countless people came and went, and many people visited the food store, but no one—literally no one—even glanced at this little puppy! Some other dogs and cats have left the platform; some of them fell asleep, but this puppy beside me is still waiting with more hope! His shining big doe eyes, little movements of his ear and nose, and his continuously wagging tail are making me a cry baby. My eyes are getting blurry by the time, but still, his hope in humanity is surprising me! Why are you so innocent? No one even cares for you here! You are not going to have food here! Why... why don't you go? Why don't you go to other places to search? Maybe... maybe you could find something from there to eat! Please go and... and... *(sobbing)* I can't help you this time! You poor little baby! I am sorry! I am... Without finishing my words, the puppy rushed outside the platform. I could not understand his sudden movement, so I was about to get up and follow him, but at that moment he returned. He is coming towards me—I mean, the food shop!—with something in his mouth. I could not see before, but now, as he is coming in front of my sight, I can see him clearly. He has some leaves in his mouth. What is he going to do with those leaves? He stands in front of me as a part of the line. As it was about to be the end of the day, the line is now getting shorter! The puppy is now a part of that short line. I was observing his movements. After some time, when it was his turn, he was wagging his tail with a wide smile and huge hope. He is now putting those leaves gently in front of the money counter. I can't believe my eyes! He was observing all those human behaviours all day long, just in the hope of having some food! Maybe for some bread and sweets! How tender they are! I can't believe this! *(in an emotional tone)*

I was so happy, but within a moment, my happiness vanished with the sudden behaviour of the shopkeeper! He did not at all praise the gentle behaviour of the puppy. He threw all the leaves and hit the puppy with a stone! Is he even a human?! What kind of behaviour is this!? Don't they have any emotions? What is wrong with them? I was about to hug that puppy, but I could not. With disbelief, the puppy is now wandering around the food stall, curling his tail inside! He is making noises as if he is trying to clarify the fact that he was not trying to harm them! He was not snatching their food; instead, he was trying to trade like the way humans do. He did not have money, so he took leaves as a medium of trade! I then kept following the puppy; he kept wandering. After some time, the guard came into my sight. He is a man in his forties, with loose trousers on him and the necklace...the necklace. I... am... I have seen it somewhere, but where? It is something that I have seen recently. I was lost in my thoughts, then, with a noise, I got back to my senses. The guard is now taking the Waste Bin to a corner. After that, he tossed all the waste food into that corner. The place is much more like a gross. He was then turning back from that place when suddenly the puppy went there and started eating food. Within a minute, the man turned back and hit the puppy with that heavy trash bin.

Noo! I am all numb! What was that? What the hell was that? Without wasting any more time, I rushed towards the puppy, but the next movement of that guard left me frozen on my spot. He picked up the trash bin from the ground, and he kept beating the puppy to death. I managed to move my stunned leg forward towards that lying puppy. After reaching there, I immediately started resisting that guard's hitting, but my existence could not help but resist him.

I turned back, started yelling and crying for help, but everybody were looking like thousands of dead souls!! Everyone was gawking at that inhumane incident, but no one—no fucking one—stepped forward to help that little baby! That fucker kept beating the puppy until he lost his life. His beautiful eyes are now filled with tears, his cute nose and ears are now cold, his wagging tail is not moving anymore, his face full of hope is now hopeless, and his spontaneous legs have no more limbs and bones. What was his fault? Why did he have to die? Why did he have to end up like this? I am crying with all my heart out, but... in front of me, a living animal with a coat of human skin is looking at the puppy with his furious red eyes and smiling continuously as if he did something good! As if that bastard won a match! But his eyes—I am known to those eyes. I know these red eyes very well! And the necklace. Then I remembered about the furry beast in the train compartment. A sudden realisation jerked me! You fucking beast! You are an inhuman beast! What did this puppy do to you? Why?? I was continuously crying out of frustration with that little dead body of that poor puppy by my side, then, with a flash, I came back to the dark world... Everything is gone once again! And still, I am crying with my knees down! What is happening with me? What is all of this? I can't take this anymore! How could they kill any life so easily with no regret? Those innocent lives! What was their fault?! Not anymore! Bring me that puppy alive. He was innocent. I can't. Please, I can't do this anymore. Please let me go. I can't take this anymore! Let me go out of here! For some time, I kept repeating the same words and continuously beating my own chest out of pain and disbelief. I am all tired now, staring at my lap, on which the puppy was lying sometimes ago. No one did anything! No one did anything! How could they? How could they be so careless? That freaking lunatic, that bastard! For some time, I kept murmuring those same words and crying my heart out! No, no, not like this! I have to get up; I have to complete the story! I have to solve the riddle! I was about to raise my hand to wipe my tears, then my eyes went on my mysterious body. My skin, my dress, everything is turning black. My body is now filled with numerous scars and many spots on my skin, and my dress is now almost black in colour. It is like I am now a complete new me. I am now slowly understanding what I was going through this morning. But the reason behind that—the reason behind everything—is still unknown. So, no more crying; I have to get up. I have to know the truth! By then, I got up and started moving towards the next compartment. Like in the past, I am now a viewer of an incident. It is a food stall in front of the gateway to a train station. It is a rainy afternoon. From my right side, a kid with torn and faded outfits who was wandering in the streets in this heavy rain sometimes ago is heading to the food stall in front of me. He is wanting food from the people at that food stall. He get several refusals, but still, he keeps touching and showing his belly and mouth to the stall keeper. He must be dying out of hunger! And also, the rain is increasing its motion. He is not wearing any warm clothes; he is all wet now! He should need something to eat in order to feel warm. After some time, I saw the stall keeper agree to give him food. The kid is happy right now, and despite being cold and hungry for days, he is jumping and clapping in happiness with his little hands. His happiness, his smiling face, is giving me happiness, but still, my smile is not shining. I don't know, but there is something I can feel from my senses, probably a bad omen or something like that. But still, I am trying to be happy with the happiness of that little boy. I am standing from a distance, and because of the rain, I can't see the clear image of everything, and honestly, I don't have any energy to go and scrutinise every detail like before. I know, somehow, how the story is going to end! But the reason why I myself am here is still unknown, and that's what my mission is! Suddenly, I saw the boy working in that stall, doing dishes, cleaning the place, and helping make foods. To know the situation, I can't help but resist myself from going there to check what is happening! Why is he working instead of eating? After entering that stall, I realised the stall keeper, who is now inside the room resting peacefully, had given a condition to this innocent little kid. Only if he would work to help the stall with cleaning or anything regarding that, only then he would get that kid some food! I am now standing with my mouth wide open! It is raining outside, the little kid is totally wet and has nothing to wear, has been hungry for many days, and is completely hopeless! Will it be a very big deal if they give him free food? Is it necessary to pay for everything every time? I could not say or do anything more than watch the kid work happily just for some food. A few times I tried to guard him from the raindrops coming from outside, but I knew I was not a good help in this appearance. A few hours have passed, and it is now raining heavily outside. The little kid is not tired but is done with his work. So now he is calling for the stall keeper: 'Master! Master? Come here, please! Master? 'What? Who is shouting at this time?' A deep voice is coming from the inside. 'Master, it's me! Look! I have done all the work, Master! 'Oh you!' By saying that, a middle-aged man with a huge, tall body is coming in front of us. When he turned on the light at the cash counter, I got to see his face. I was stunned!! The man with an eating disorder!! What? What is he going to do this time? I instantly rush towards the kid out of fear! No! It can't be! Don't kill him! Don't kill him! Don't dare to touch him! He is a good soul! Don't touch him! *(Weeping constantly)* I am trying to protect that kid by hugging him, but it was of no use for that time! He did not kill him instead…

'You finished all the work?' 'Yes, Master.' 'Hmm... Alright! Now you can leave.' 'Ma...Master' 'What? You have done everything, right? Now leave. 'Master, my food, Master...' 'What food? What are you talking about?' 'Master, my food!! You told me to work if I wanted to eat food! Master, I worked hard!! I did everything! Look there, master. I washed all dishes, I cleaned everything... I did everything. I did more than you told me, Master!! *(sobbing)* Master, I am dying of hunger!! Please let me eat something! I'm very much hungry, Master.'

'I have never told anything like that. I thought you came for helping hands, but you are a beggar! Tell me the truth! Did you steal something from here? Tell me, you son of a bitch! You are a thief. I knew it before!' 'What are you saying, Master? I did not steal anything! Why would I do that? Please, Master, give me my food!' 'You son of a bitch! Leave right now!' By that, the shopkeeper kicks the crying little poor kid by grabbing his hair from the shop. Before I could process properly, the light was gone, and the darkness of the compartment and the darkness of the story left me numb with shock! I don't know what to say, and I don't know what to do. But I am dying slowly from inside, and I now can feel that. All these actions and all these inhumane behaviours are making me emotionless! I am now on my way to becoming gloomy. I can feel that something is happening wrong inside me, and it is not at all waiting for me or my permission. My body is not working by my choice. After that, I started walking again and witnessed three compartments depicting three different crimes! In the next compartment, I witnessed a poor, hungry family roaming on the platform in search of some help; probably they were in need of food or money. They were looking tired and done with their neglected lives. They were looking here and there in search of someone to help them while sitting in a small, dirty corner of the platform. At that time, a fat woman, with some luggage carried by her maid, was passing by the poor family. The fat woman was wearing a saree, covered with many gold jewellery pieces, and in her hand there was a tiffin box. She was eating something, and by looking at that, the young kid of the poor family could not resist himself and pulled her *aanchal* (the ending part of saree) in search of food. The fat lady looked back at them and kicked the poor boy's face harshly. The little boy was crying; the family felt insulted and was crying terribly, but the fat woman not only avoided them but also tossed all her food in front of them and smashed them with her shoes. She had many things to give that poor family, but still, she gave them her inhumane arrogance! After that, I witnessed two different compartments with almost the same story. The setting for both of the stories is the gateway to the train. When the train arrives and when it is the time of its departure, the emergency and rush of every human being come into existence! Every time, it is the same story for everyone! They don't look at others, they don't care for others, and they tend to ignore everything around them just to place themselves inside the train! Of course, they have to behave in that way. After all, it is their last chance for life! Maintaining the same urge, a boy was about to catch the train. He was at the doorway. When the train started moving, there was another person who was hanging from the gate of the train. As the boy in his teenage years was the only one who was standing next to the door after getting into the train, the hanging man asked him for help. But the teenage boy could not listen to him as he was listening to music by plugging in his earphone. The man was continuously asking for help. There was a time when the boy looked at that man for real, but still, he did not help him and ignored him. As a result, when the train increased its speed, the hanging man lost his balance over himself and ended up dying on the spot, and even his one leg was brutally chopped by the wheels of the train. Like that in the next story, a girl pushed a woman to death while both of them were hanging from the gateway. As a result, the woman lost her life with her body chopped into several pieces and spreading all around. Without any shame, without any humanity, the girl kept standing on the gateway, guarding the doorknob as if it were her own property. I, the same as before, could not do anything but look at them with a speechless, broken heart.

5.

Degradation of Morality

After finishing all these things, I am now standing in front of a dark, black place. Once again, everything is gloomy, and once again, I am all alone, but the only difference is that I am now fully immersed in this extreme darkness, as if the darkness has consumed me. Though the place near my chest, or more precisely, over my heart, is still alive with its white colour, except for that, I am now in a black dress, and my body is all covered with several bruises, cuts, and other bloody wounds. I am not worried right now. I don't know why! Should I be worried? Should I, or should I not? I can't sense anything. What is happening to me? I looked here and there and finally found the doorway. Without thinking or knowing anything, I kept following that way. I am walking, but why am I feeling pain all over my body? Why is it too difficult to walk? My back is hurting, and the unbearable pain in my back has reached its peak! And... and my eyes—there is something in my eyes. By that, I was about to rub my eyes with my hand, and then suddenly I noticed something. Some people are sitting far from me. I am getting an unclear image of them as I am standing far from them. To know who they are, I keep moving until I reach there and see those horrible beast-like creatures sitting all together in the same place. They are looking at me; I am also looking at them, but... I don't know! I don't know why they look different in my eyes. As if the entire background is blurry but only their faces are looking clear. What kind of sight is this? I could not understand anything, and then my eyes went to all the creatures present in the place. They were all calling me to come to them, and some of them were making body language to call me to sit next to them. I went there and sit at the seat, which is situated in the middle of everyone present there. So, I am now in the middle of all the criminals, and my eyes are now witnessing the heartless bastards. I should be bursting out of anger, but... but... why? Why am I sitting like this? Why am I doing nothing? Why is there no emotion working within me? Why! What is the problem? What is wrong with me? From my eyes, some drops of tears start rolling down, but ironically, my face does not share any emotion of sorrow, anger, or anything else.

'You are crying, Beatrix!' says the fat, jelly-like woman. "I love watching you cry, Beatrix."

"Beatrix is crying."

"I love this."

"Beatrix is crying."

"Beatrix crying! No more smiles; smiles no more."

One by another, they start mocking me! They are making fun of my emotions! Emotions that I... I cannot even feel! But why are they loving me enough to cry? Why are they saying all these things? I thought, and aloud I said, "Why? Why do you love watching me cry? Why does my sorrow give you happiness?"

They kept quiet for some time. The silence is awkward and makes me less patient. They are not saying anything and are continuously looking at each other. Their faces are still like statues! With the hope of getting an answer, I break the silence.

"Why are you not answering now? You said you loved watching me cry! So tell me, why did you say that? Wh..."

Without letting my words go, the furry beast yells at me, "Because you are the reason, Beatrix! You are the reason!"

And then, one by one,

"You are the problem."

"Yes, yes, it's you! You are the reason!"

"Beatrix is the problem."

"You are the reason."

They are turning into a noisy mess, so I end up shouting out loud, "The reason for what?"

Everyone stops. The chaotic mess is now once again quiet!

"The reason for what? Explain it to me clearly! I am the reason for what?"

"You are the reason for our misfortune."

"You are the reason for our situation."

"Beatrix is the reason."

"You are the one, Beatrix."

"They are the reason for our misfortune."

"What? Who are they?" I asked curiously. "What are you all talking about? Who are they? Who is the reason for your misfortune? Including me, who are they?" I asked them, but suddenly I noticed all the gloomy, emotionless faces were now getting facial expressions! Not like the same as before; their faces are now getting bigger, and... and they are now groaning as if they are all predators. Predators from the wild. The furry beast is now getting fluffier and bigger than before. The man with an eating disorder is now all covered by his unexpectedly huge belly! The one-ear-chopped boy now has a longer tongue, and his head is now bigger than his entire body! The fat lady has now turned into a big jelly ball and the pregnant man is now all red in anger, and his belly is now pregnant with countless babies, which are visible from here. The sight is dangerous. Suddenly, the compartment is covered with a huge flow of wind. The place is now one shade darker! I notice all the eyes of the predators are not on me; they are looking at the doorway. So I thought to turn back and see what was right there! I was about to turn back, but then... "Beatrix, here you are! I told you; we are all waiting for you!" The teenage girl with half a body has come by floating in the air, and her half-body has now turned into a long tail floating. A broken part of the doorknob of the gate of the train is still in her hand. After floating all around me for some time, she finally settled herself on top of the fat lady, her tail now covering the fat lady.

"You are the reason for our situation; they are responsible for us," she says.

"You have to be clear with your opinions," I said loudly. "Who are they? I am responsible for you, but why? And who are the others? Who is responsible for you?"

"The hungry boy," says the man with an eating disorder, and then, one by one:

"The puppy," says the furry beast.

"The poor family," says the fat lady.

"The pregnant woman," says the pregnant, big-belly man.

"The hanging man," says the one-ear-chopped teenage boy.

"The lady at the door," says the flying teenage girl. I am all stunned! Did they all just talk about those who were the victims of their wrong deeds? Did they really talk about those to whom they acted inhumanely? Did they talk about them who were betrayed by themselves? I could not resist my anger. My emotions are now coming back slowly. I am slowly regaining my senses. "What are you talking about? They are the reason for your misfortune! Are they responsible for all of this? How could you even spell their name when you are all the ones who were?" I could not complete my words and ended up being scared, as the furry beast almost came in front of me and was about to hit me. My eyes are all closed now! What a horrible sight it was! The beast is all in his rising anger! My heart is beating continuously! I am afraid now! Though it was a relief that my senses had come back, I was terrified by the sudden action of that furry beast! With slow movements, I open my eyes to see if anything has come to its normal state or if the beast is still standing there, but when I turn my head to my front, I notice something unexpected! A furry beast is fighting with all his power against an aura, against a light that has been surrounding me. A blue light that is now guarding me. I could not understand what just happened and is still happening! After some time, the furry beast got tired and sat back in his seat. I thought I should not behave rudely; I should talk to them gently, or maybe the situation would be more furious! I take a gulp and try not to make any sound, but the silence is very deep, so the sound of my gulp creates an awkward impact. I should now start talking to them! "Umm... why... why do you think they are the reason behind your misfortune? I mean, do you remember anything?" I gently threw the question to all these creatures present there. They are now looking at each other, so I think I should choose someone among them. "Anyone of you can answer! You, you, the flying girl! What do you think? What did the woman at the door do to you? Can you remember?"

"Why won't I?!" The girl says, "I can remember everything! Everything is picturized in front of my eyes."

"Okay, alright, tell me. Tell me what she did to you."

"I was in a rush; I had to catch that train," she answers. "But you caught that! Did you not?"

"I caught the train."

"Then what was the matter?"

"That woman came from behind. We both were hanging and struggling to stand on the gate, and we both stood there successfully!"

"Then what? Everything was solved, wasn't it?"

"No, not at all! I loved to stand in front of the gate, but that day I couldn't do that because that lady was standing there instead of me."

"Then?"

"So, I pushed her from the train!"

"So you pushed someone to death because you wanted to fulfill your desire?"

I was about to say many things, but for that time, I remained silent to mind the circumstances.

"And because of that lady, I ended up like this."

"You murdered that lady!! And you are accusing her and making her the villain here?"

"She died instantly on the spot. Her body was chopped into parts! After some days, I lost my legs in an accident, which was unpredictable! I was on public transport, and suddenly that transport lost control over the brake, and it tossed! Everybody on that transport was safe except me! My legs were chopped down as a result of that accident! For a few days, I was under treatment, but the condition was getting worse day by day! Doctors said it was necessary for my health to chop down my lower body in order to survive. But during the surgery, the doctor made a mistake, and I died with no life in me!"

I slightly smiled after listening to her story. She noticed, but I didn't care. "And you... you are the reason, Beatrix," said the girl, but I did not care about her talking and instantly moved to another creature to know their perspective. It was the turn of a pregnant man, who said the pregnant lady was the reason behind his misfortune! The reason behind that is unbelievable! The lady was bothering him to take his seat, and according to him, the lady was abnormal, and it was her fault to come to the public with her abnormality—her pregnancy! After some days of that lady's death, the man caught a disease and got a womb. A tumour in his stomach which was getting bigger, looking like a womb. The pain was too much for him to cope with! At last, he died of horrible pain! He accused the pregnant lady of spreading the disease. I was speechless by his opinion, but it was such a pleasure knowing the result! Truly it was! After that, one by one, they shared their opinion. It went like the man with an eating disorder was accusing the poor kid of being responsible for him because, after betraying him, a few days later he noticed some changes in his behaviour. He was getting hungry more often, and the more he was eating, the more he was getting hungry from time to time! One day, because of overeating, he died. The fat woman was accusing that the poor family was the reason for her to end like that, because a few days after her encounter with that poor family, she was hospitalised as she caught food poisoning, but after that, her entire body started changing forms. And at the end, it formed into a terrible-looking shape, and her skin was infected badly. Out of pain and all the uncertainty, doctors decided to kill her, because if she did not, she would eventually die, but in unbearable, incompatible pain. Then the teenage boy said his ear had been chopped because of the man who was hanging from the train. I asked him, "Why did you not save him? He was right beside you! Right?" "He was irritating me, and there were other people there, so why did they not help him? Why is the man only disturbing me?" "Because you were the only one who was beside him." "I don't care; he was interrupting my music listening." I remain silent! Then I asked, "Then what happened to you next?"

"A few days later, I was on the same platform, about to catch a train. I was just like before, standing next to the door, listening to music. It was raining outside, and the gate was open. Everyone on the train was calling me, but I could not hear as my ear was blocked because of my earphone. Suddenly, the train tilted to my side because of its sudden jerk! I don't know how I slid from the train and caused spot death!"

"And you think that happened because of that man?"

"Or what? He was the one and only reason!"

I smiled. I just smiled because they just didn't make any sense. Now, at the very last, I turn my face to that furry beast, to whom I have plenty of questions! He was the one whose behaviour jerked my senses and made all my emotions almost dead.

"And you, Mr. What is your reason? Who made you end up like this... this furry beast?" I intentionally made the last words sound creepy.

The furry beast is now looking at me with anger, and after some time, he replies, "The dog."

"The dog? That little puppy?!" I repeated his words.

"Yes. That furry beast!"

"Beast? Huh? Wow! And how did he make you end up like this? How far I can remember, you killed him to death! Did you not?"

"Yes, I did! He was annoying me! Those furry beasts are nothing more than gross to our society."

"What did you say? Society? Okay, now carry on! What happened to you exactly?"

"I was a spiritual person. I loved worshipping all the deities! But these beasts are gross! They are making society nasty! And deities love holiness, and these beasts are not holy at all! That's why I hate them the most! And when I saw that beast making the place dirty, I was angry and when I got my chance, I killed him! Cause those who are gross, are meant to be cleared! But many days later, I was in a temple. It was the rainy season, and the situation was running bad. Because of harsh weather, the rain did not stop, and the continuous rain caused a sudden flood. Everyone within the temple started running towards the exit, and I was left behind as I believed in the God who would save me no matter what! After all, I devoted my entire existence to him. Within a few moments, water started coming into the temple. Then I was worried and tried to escape the temple, but somehow the door got locked, and I was screaming for help! But no one came to save me. No one. My god, my saviour, was in front of me, but still, he was silent! After that, without letting me know, everything got destroyed, including me and my god. When I woke up, I was over some rocks, and other rocks were over me! I was in so much pain that my one leg was pressed by a huge pillar. In that unbearable pain, I was dying, calling for help, but there was no one. I was praying to God, but my god was also there, lying beside me, destroyed into countless pieces! After some time, I ended my battle to be alive. My pain, my death—everything happened because of that dog! That furry beast!" "You are the furry beast!" I did not wait for him to finish his words and started yelling.

"You are!! You all are the beast right here! How dare you!! How could you even tell your own fault with so much glory? You are the one who committed the crime! You are the one who neglected someone's life! That little kid! He was a child! A goddamn child dying of hunger! He even worked continuously with a smile on his face, with the hope of having food, and what did he get? Betrayal?? That poor family, what did they do? They were hopeless, but they did not deserve that much insult! The hanging man, the lady in front of the door—they were just existing, and you killed them! You let them die just to fulfil your own satisfaction! The pregnant lady! Did she really deserve to be insulted? How could you talk to her like that? Pregnancy is a disease?? NO, sir! You are the one who has the disease! Disease in your heart. Disease in your mind. I am done with your gross-like mentality!! And you, the furry beast! That puppy was pure. He had the purest heart! He eagerly waited all day long and did not behave badly, just for some food. And what were you going to do with that leftover waste food? Huh? Were you going to create something by that? Or were you going to eat that yourself? You even threw that! Right? At the end? Then what the hell was your problem with that innocent life? You killed a speechless life! All the blood and all the innocence were lying there in front of you! Weren't you afraid? Or was that the way you worshipped? Was that a part of your prayer? Then how could you do that? God doesn't live in temples or anywhere else, rather God lives in everything and in everyone. You just need a good eye and a pure soul to find that. You all killed your God that day! And... now! You are blaming those innocent lives who were the victims of your misdeeds! You limbless bastard!! Were you even human? Where was your humanity? Your morality? Your spirituality? You learned all this from your holy god?? Your attitude, even your beliefs, have now become a total zero! You are..."

I stopped while talking. Their faces, with no emotion, are now getting bigger. They are extending their sizes, and by that view, I am now feeling a weird, cold chill run down my spine. Suddenly, one of them starts saying my name.

"Beatrix! Beatrix!"

And following him, others go like one by one.

"There it is! There it is!"

"Beatrix, we were waiting for you."

"We want you, Beatrix."

"We want that."

"Come here."

"We are now tired."

"You are responsible, Beatrix. They are responsible."

"Come to us; let us have it."

"We were waiting for so long! Come here."

They are now coming closer to me; their big faces and their horrible presence are now surrounding me slowly. They are still blaming those innocent souls as if their soul also died at the time of death! Or... or there was no soul in them while they were alive. There is so much darkness within them! The darkness is much darker than the compartment, the coach, and the train itself! I am now all trapped by these creatures. But the place... it is like... the place is also getting narrower, as if it also tries to eat me. "Beatrix, you are the reason!"

"But why am I the reason? What are they going to have from me?" Within a few moments, they came in front of me and were about to touch me! Their bloody nails and their big red eyes had trapped me! But then, in a flash of light, everyone fell out with a sudden jerk! My eyes were closed out of fear, but now after opening them, I can see the light is too bright to make them suffer like lunatics. They are all howling!

I look at my body, and immediately I am shocked! The light is coming from my chest—more precisely, my heart! What is happening to me? What is this light, and what does it mean? I could not understand anything. Then I see the characters trying to fight against the light and trying to come to me once again. Simultaneously, I notice there is a door that is only visible because of the light. Without any further delay, I started to run and follow the path that was guided by that unknown light.

I started running, but the more I was running, the more afraid I was becoming! Every wall of this coach is getting narrower, as if it is going to smash me! It is not willing to let me go. The creatures are also following me as if there is no tomorrow. The long wide view of this compartment will look like a straight line in no time. I can only hear the noise of howling and growling. Without any thoughts of anything else, I kept running. I was running as fast as possible until

I saw a big, broken mirror.

I stopped and was amazed at looking at my replica in the mirror. It is like the image I saw while entering this train, but it is much more horrible than before! The replica of mine is staring at me from the mirror with the same emotionless, gloomy face as those creatures! While taking their name, their replica popped up there on the mirror, out of the blue! I got startled and turned back out of fear, but what is this? There is no one here right behind me.

So I turned again to the mirror, and the creatures are now coming nearer in the mirror! Even my replica is acting negatively weird on that mirror. All of them, including me, are smiling at me. The place is getting narrower and blurrier; the mirror is getting bigger; the replicas are now trying to come out of the mirror; they are laughing creepily; and now the growling sound of the creatures is coming closer. The sound of their footsteps is now even louder. There is total chaos in my head! I can't understand anything! I don't know what to do. That situation was eating me emotionally, and I could not take it anymore.

I closed my eyes, yelled out louder, and hit the mirror with my bare hands! There was a sudden bright light, and all I could hear was the cracking sound of that mirror.

6.

Truth Unfolds

I am feeling dizzy. Ah! What just happened to me? What was that sound and the light? Was that coming from me? I look at my chest out of disbelief! What was that? What was its purpose? Ugh! My head aches! And my entire body aches! My legs! It's painful! With that, I slowly opened my eyes. For some time, I could not see anything. Everything is white. Where am I? After some moments of observation, I got to understand that I was back at the station! The same platform from where I started the journey! Everything is the same! Then... then did I manage to get out of the train? Really? I am out of that weird train! I did it! Yes! Finally, I did it! I am now off the train! What a relief! I was happy because of my successful escape, but then I noticed I was sitting on the platform floor, as if I fell there from somewhere. I make an effort and get up from the floor. No! I was wrong! The sudden realisation hit me. The place is not all the same as before! Silence, which was the main attraction of this platform, is now missing. I can hear some voices from a distance. It's a female voice. No, no! It is a male voice! Oh! Now I can hear some kids' voices. I turn my face to that side and start to walk in that direction, following the voices. After walking for some steps, I can hear a male voice and the kids' voices. Then, with more steps, the voice of a woman! The laughing sound and the playing sound of the kids are now audible in my ear! The curiosity buried within me is now letting me increase my speed to follow the voices. After returning from such a dark place with an evil vibe, now the positive sound of happiness and the happy, smiling voices are motivating me to move forward! Despite having all the pain and being covered with countless bruises, within a few more steps, I witnessed an indescribable happiness showering in my heart. A little puppy is running towards me with a happy face, a very wide smile, and those happy little moves by those tiny, cute legs with a wagging fluffy tail! My face is now shining with happiness and sharing the brightest smile I have had in a while. The puppy came in front of me and gifted me its love by jumping on me with a happy gesture. I am also showing my love for a lot of pets. It is an adorable male puppy, but why is he giving me the vibe that I know him? "Do I know you, sweetie? What is this feeling inside me? You are too much known to me," I asked with my dog voice. The puppy smiles back at me and nods his head as he gives me his approval to know each other. Then, I don't know what he thought, and all of a sudden, he runs towards somewhere, out of sight. I don't have a clue where he went or why! Doesn't he like me? Did I hurt him somewhere? I mean, as far as I remember, I didn't do anything! Did I touch him inappropriately? No, no! I did not! Then why did he leave? Why he... I stopped overthinking and decided to move on towards the voices. I have to follow them. Where is this positive voice coming from in this barren land? I have to find out. With that thinking, I stepped forward and was about to leave the place, but then, surprisingly, I saw that puppy running towards me with the same happiness on his face. However, this time it seems like he has something in his mouth. I don't know what this is, and from this distance, it is even very hard to make a guess! I kneel down, waiting for that puppy until he comes to me. I was smiling once again, then suddenly all faded up, and I lost my speech and became all numb. The puppy has come with leaves in his mouth, with the same innocence and surprising intelligence. I am no longer in confusion. It is clear like water; in front of me is the puppy of that story, the victim of that horrible, inhumane activity! I could not hold back my emotions anymore. Tears are rolling down from my watery eyes; my emotions are now showering and coming in front of the world! That puppy gave those leaves to me, and that made me burst out of tears. I immediately hugged him, and now I am crying while hugging him. "I am sorry, baby! What happened to you was not the result of your good deeds. You did not deserve that, baby! I'm sorry I couldn't help you at the time. I am sorry! Please forgive me, you little poor thing. You deserved much more. Sorry, honey, they couldn't understand your purity! Sorry, baby, I am sorry! *(sobbing repeatedly)* You pure soul, you deserve much, much more! I am sorry for their behaviour. They are blind. They only see what they want to see, and if there is anything they don't want to see, then that is simply impurity for them. They are making their own rules, which will surely end them one day. I am sorry! "During this time, I am feeling some cold drops dripping on my shoulder, and it didn't take me long to understand what was going on. By kissing his forehead, I am now slowly caressing his head. "You were hungry! I am sorry for that. They didn't even pay any attention to you. I am sorry for that! You were waiting for the entire day just for some food! I am so sorry for that, honey! You were extremely genuine, honey! I am sorry for that! The waste foods were in front of you, but without losing patience, you were waiting. I am sorry for that! I am extremely sorry, honey! They let you die, and they enjoyed your death. I am very much sorry! Please forgive me. I wish I could meet you in your lifetime! Please, baby, don't cry. Don't be sad! We will meet in the next life, okay? We will eat a lot of food, and we will have our shelter. We will have our own home! Everything will be comfortable, and we will have a lot of fun. You will love your life, baby! Please wait for me!! I will make you love your afterlife. I turn the puppy's face at my front and say, 'You will wait for me! Won't you?' The puppy nods his approval. I give him a warm smile. We both are now crying, but no more in pain. Then we decide to move further, but within a moment, we meet a happy-looking kid with a good-to-go comfy outfit over his healthy body. At first, I couldn't recall him, but then when he asked, 'Remember me, Beatrix?' I was stunned! That was the boy from the food shop. "Are you that boy? Oh my god! You are looking way different. You have totally upgraded yourself," I say with extreme happiness. "How did you make it? Um, I mean, I don't want to offend you, but I am just curious. How did you escape your past?"

"I didn't." The boy's answer now makes me frown. "Am... wo... what do you mean by that?"

"That was not the only time I was rejected by so many people in my life. At first, my parents left me; their poorness made them reject me. I was abandoned on a lonely street! The four-year-old me had to go and wait in front of many places in search of food. The sense of being abandoned was much more painful, but sometimes I had to get up myself, stop crying, and look for food. I had to stand in front of someone's house, someone's store, someone's food stall, and someone's workplace. I begged them to give me food; even though I was totally alright with leftover food, no one gave me anything. Still, I had to wait and stand like a living stone just in hope of being noticed by the right person who could understood my pain, but that right person never came! Sometimes the hunger went so intense that I had to look for food in the dustbin. I even wanted to start my life again by working to get food, but people like that shopkeeper crushed my dreams with their educated legs! That night, because of the continuous rainfall, the roads were slippery. After that incident, I was crying ridiculously hard out of hunger, and I was also so done with my life. It was hard to see anything on the road, so I kept running in search of a shelter. While running on that road, a truck appeared unexpectedly and smashed all my limbs and all my hopes over that road. I could not make it, Beatrix!" There is a small drop of tears shining at the corner of his eyes like a spotless pearl. He is sharing his warm smile with me. He is still in hope after his death, and here I am now, a total crying mess! Why do all the good people turn up like this? I thought, and loudly I said, "I am sorry! I know it does not make any sense, and yes, it now sounds like bullshit, but please forgive me, and if possible, forgive them! Please forgive your past! It was not your fault to be born poor; it was not your fault to be abandoned; it was not your fault to feel hungry; and it was not your fault to end up like that. It was their fault; they did not understand you! They did not want to listen to your words; they did not want to listen to your story! It was their fault! They were self-centred! They were selfish! It was their fault! You had the right to dream big. Everyone does! No one had or has the right to smash them! You will be happy in your next life. Please don't be sad! Plea..."

By cutting my upcoming words, he replies, "No, Beatrix, I am not sad! Look at me! Am I looking like a sad person to you? I am happy, Beatrix! I have no regrets about my past! They did what they had to do. People are the same, Beatrix! All humans are born with equal emotions and an equal mind-set! Everyone is not born good or bad. Everything is equal, Beatrix, just like the way life is beautiful! It is just your perspective on how you see the world! It is just your choice to live kind and embrace the purity of your soul, or just live like a living dead soul. Because of my bad past, I don't want to stop my dreams! When I died, for some time I was very angry and tried to haunt and scare people, but then one day I met another kid living just like my past. From that moment on, I could not keep up with my anger. From that realisation, my life and my mentality changed, and I decided to be kind to someone. Now, Beatrix, I am the guardian angel of that little boy. He knows about me, and he accepts me, and we are living happily, however we are living."

I am speechless! How can someone who ended his life because of the brutal side of humanity, who was the victim of such a horrible incident, think about life like this? I don't have any power to speak any further; my throat is all heavy right now! How the power of positive mentality can cause such remarkable differences between people! I was all lost in the words of that little boy when, to my surprise, one by one, all the victims of those stories came, and the poor family are now looking magnificent with their great health. Then, the hanging man and the lady in front of the door are also coming slowly. All of them are happy and totally alright with their health; all of them are recovering from their brutal past. The poor family is also dead, according to their description. All of the family members attempted suicide after some days. The fat lady was from a wealthy, powerful family. She misused her power and filed a case against them. They did not have money to fight for their own. From public insults, repeated police inquiries, and threat calls, their lives became a living hell, and over all these things, they didn't have food or energy to cope with all that brutality. So one day, the entire family planned to end their lives, and as a result, together, inside the public toilet of the platform, they hanged themselves. The most pathetic thing is the fact that there was an infant in the family! What was her fault? What did that baby do to end her life like this? They have gone through so many things, but still, they are standing in front of me with a great gesture of positivity and happiness. I was talking to them and listening to their stories, and then I saw some people coming. When the distance became too short to measure, all I could see was a woman with a child coming towards us. The woman is talking to her baby. That is a girl with a pretty princess dress! They are talking and laughing as if I am watching a happy picture. The mother is that pregnant lady that I can see, but the child... who is this baby girl? "Beatrix! Here you are!"

When they finally reach us, the mother calls me with a wide, welcoming, warm smile on her face. I am now shocked; I don't know what to say to her. The amount of pain she endured on that bus was unbearable, and I was watching that but could not do anything! I could not stand by her side when she was being insulted by that bastard! I am now facing that person who was insulted because of her pregnancy, and I could not do anything for her! How can I bring my gaze to her? It's a shame for me! "So what I heard was not wrong! Beatrix is present among us for real! Nice to meet you, Beatrix! We were waiting for you," she says. "Waiting for me?" I repeat.

"Yes, we were waiting for you."

"Bu...but I mean, I am sorry! I am really stunned! So it's kind of hard to say anything!"

"Wait! Wait! Take a moment! Take a deep breath! Feel at ease! You don't need to be sorry! I know why you are behaving like this. Please don't worry that much!"

"I am sorry... I am really sorry... That man was a bastard! Whatever he said was complete bullshit! Please don't mind that! Pregnancy is the best gift of every mother's life. It is not a freaking disease! It is a fortune to be able to give birth to a new life. It's a topic to celebrate! The celebration is to let the world know that you are going to be the creator of the best art form, a life! There is no need to hide it or staying and resting at home! I am very sorry for each and every word that bastard told you."

"So what I heard was right. What I heard about you is totally right! It is too worthy to meet you in person, Beatrix," she remarks as a reply to my talking. I don't know what the reason behind the name is, but it is now becoming a part of my own existence! To hear the name 'Beatrix' is giving me pleasure in my ears. It is now giving me happiness! I smile as a reply to her good words, and after that, without wasting any time, I say, "And who is this little beauty? Hi, princess! Are you with her?" I ask while looking at the girl child.

"Mumma! Say hello to Beatrix, aunty," she told that little girl, and I am left in shock.

"Mumma? You mean??" "Yes! My baby!" My heart is racing fast

right now. That baby was dead with her on that day. That baby is all grown up. A little princess. I don't know how long I can hold back my tears." I was a single mother, Beatrix. After my marriage, my husband's family forced me to undergo a sex determination test as they were dying to have a baby boy. Then, after doing the test, they again forced me to give up on my baby and do an abortion, as the result was a girl. When I announced my decision to have the child no matter what, they started beating me and making death threats. One day, they were even going to kick my belly to let that baby die. After that incident, I left the place and decided to have the child and be a single mother for her. It was very hard for me to find a place to live and earn money to buy medicine and food for the baby. As a single woman, I even got harassed many times, but still, I strongly maintained all things single-handed! That day, I was returning from the store after buying things for my baby, who was about to be delivered in a couple of days. At that time, my entire body was in pain, and to move a little was like an impossible job for me, but still, for the baby, I went there. Also, I had no one to get help from; as a result, I had to do everything by myself. But that incident on the bus—the words of that man reminded me of my past! And it was really hard for me to even think about that! I thought I was strong, but maybe I was not strong enough to bear that much pressure and ended up losing my opportunity to be a mother. That baby died with me; all my sacrifice, my dream, all my hard work, and my entire existence died that day with us, Beatrix! But don't worry; there is no need to blame them. Maybe education is just a competition these days, so as a result, it is really hard to be educated at the end of the day! Don't worry, Beatrix; I am happy. In fact, now I am the happiest person ever because I am now the proud mother of this little princess. To spend time with her, from smiling with her to crying with her, is my greatest pleasure, Beatrix. I named her 'Courage' as she was, she is, and she will always be my biggest courage in every situation."

I am sobbing continuously and don't have any words to describe my feelings. I slowly look at Courage; she is now smiling and waving her hands to me. "Courage! That's the finest name for you," I remark. Immediately, Courage walks forward and holds my hand. My heart is now racing faster than before! It is an indescribable feeling. Those little hands, with a lot of purity and happiness, are now making me happy and feel positive. But when I touch her back, I look at my hands. What about the wounds? All the bruises are gone now! Is it for real? I am getting back to my normal self! I was happy and surprised at the same time, but then I became even more surprised when I noticed a bag hanging from my left shoulder. What was not at all with me all the time? "What is this?" I unintentionally shouted out loud, which even made them curious. "What are you talking about, Beatrix?" asks the mother. "I mean, what is this bag? From where on Earth did it come?" "What's wrong with your bag, Beatrix? And why are you so surprised?" asks the kid boy.

"I have heard about it, so it is that bag," says the man of the poor family.

"It is not my bag! It just appeared now! Out of the blue! It was not there with me! It is not my..." Without finishing my words, I just say, "Is it my bag?" I don't know what happened to me, but somehow, I accepted the bag as mine, but in reality, it was not there from the beginning.

"Beatrix, what is inside your bag this time?" the kid asks with innocence.

"Open it, Beatrix! Let us see," says the hanging man.

Because of the repeated request, I opened the bag and found many foods, money, a water bottle, and a first aid box. How can this be possible? There were all these things inside this bag all the time, and I didn't feel them. And even the bag's weight should be much heavier, as if it contains many things! Then why is it this lightweight?

"Bu, but what am I going to do with all these things?" After saying that, I look at all the people around me, and then it becomes really clear for me what to do with all that stuff. At the very beginning, I offered some food to that little puppy, but he did not eat the full meal. After that, I offered money, food, and water to the others, but they did not take them all.

"Why don't you take it? You were in need of all these, right?"

"But we are not in need of any materialistic things now! It is a great fortune for us to have something from you, Beatrix, and we really don't want to miss this blessing! That's why we took only a small amount. We are really lucky to have that from you, Beatrix. But there are many people who need this more than us. So go and help them. We got to meet you; we got to talk to you; that's enough for us! And we are very thankful for that! Now go ahead! They are waiting for you." With such disbelief, I moved forward but didn't know whether to go. Then I got help from the cutest helper. The little puppy is now leading me to my next destination with his happy walks and wagging tail. I was confused, but now it is like a happy walk for me because of this little happy energy beside me.

Within a few more steps, I visited many street dogs, cats, some kids abandoned on the platform, some old people left alone on the station, and many more. With respect and care, I distributed all the things among them. They have all regained their long-lost energy once again. They gifted me love and warm hugs. All the time, that puppy was there for me. He is like my biggest supporter right now! It took me some good hours to give food, money, water bottles, and medicine to all of them on the platform.

After finishing my work, I was about to turn my back to return, but then I felt a tug on my dress! When I looked down, I saw the puppy tugging at the lower end of my dress, and he was trying to lead me again somewhere. I look up; there is no one left on the platform. Then, what is he trying to do? Where is he leading me? I don't know anything, but still, I decide to follow him. We walked for a couple of minutes. After reaching the place, I saw that white bench! That white bench, from where all the things started! It has now turned back to its original hue. There is no spot, no darkness on it. I can now understand what is going to come next! I can sense everything. The puppy is now bidding his goodbye to me. I also wished goodbye to him with a lot of pets and kisses! He stood there and started howling in a good tone, and I am now moving forward to my final destination. But the more I am moving, the more the bench looks like something different! Though it is kind of suspicious, somehow, I can't sense any evil right now! I have a smile on my face, and it is a true smile. That is making my inner self calm down. After reaching there, I stopped for some time, closed my eyes, and felt the place for one last time.

"Beatrix, we will meet in the next life."

"Beatrix, we will meet in the next life."

They are repeating their words from a distance, and the dog is still howling. I take a deep breath. "Yes, we will meet." With that, I lay down there. It is so comfortable here! There is so much positivity! I am able to breathe properly! There is no more pain! My legs are now all rested! My heart, my head—everything is free right now! There is no tension, no confusion, no brutality, no life and no death! There is no more chaos. Everything is peaceful here. I am happy once again, and this happiness is making my entire existence rest at ease! Everything is pleasant. I am all at ease!

~End of Beatrix's POV~

With that, the box closed with a beautiful, elegant flowers arranged on the top of it.

~Luna Hope (1963–1984)~

7.

A New Hope

"Sir, that's not the end. We can do it even better. Please trust us! Please, sir! One last chance! I promise you, we will definitely make you happy this time! Please, sir!"

"Okay, fine! One last chance! If you won't be able to come here and present me with a real good story, then you'll be fired with your entire team! Got it? Now leave! I have some bigger fish to fry."

"Thank you. Thank you so much, sir! We will not disappoint you this time."

(continuous sound of whispering)

"Hey, guys, keep quiet! The boss is coming. The meeting with the client is over."

"Shhh! Don't make any noise! Boss is in a really bad mood!" *(advises an employee)*

"Ahh! What a loss!" Throwing the papers in front of the team, the boss yelled out loud. "What are you guys doing? You... you are of no use! Totally useless! In three months, what have we done? Nothing! Totally nothing. Zero progress. Are you all listening to me?

Zero progress! Now, note it. I am giving you all one last chance. Oh! How can I give it when I am given one last dance from the client? One last chance, guys! If you can't make it, we will all be fired, and this team will be of no use."

There's an awkward, pin-drop silence in the room. No one is even willing to say anything to the boss.

"Please team! Please cover some real good stories this time. It is really a do-or-die condition. If you don't come up with a really good story within one week, then there will be no hope to survive. This team, including your and my job, will be gone. Therefore, I am requesting you."

"Bu... but boss, one week is really a short period of time. Finding a story, then doing paperwork—all these things are really impossible in just one week." Some of the employees dare to say that in front of the boss, and other employees are also supporting their statement.

"Yes, boss! One week is really a short period of time to do all these things for the entire team."

"Then divide yourselves into sub-teams and go search for new stories. And about the paperwork? I will also join you to do that. At first, go find yourselves some good stories," the boss advises, and suddenly the dull, confused faces of all the employees seem delightful with a new hope!

"Let me divide you all into sub-teams. Employee 1, Employee 2, and Employee 3 are under Team A. In Team B, employees 4, 5, and 6. Employees 7, 8, and 9 are under Team C. And Employee 10 and Employee 11, you guys are with me under Team D."

Without listening to the rest, all the employees burst into excitement. "Boss, you will work with us this time?"

"Yes, of course! We have only one week. If we don't work together, then we will be in real danger!"

"Boss, you are the best!"

"Best of all time!" says all of them.

"Okay, okay, now focus on our project. Listen, team, we have to be really quick! Team A, Team B, and Team C, you guys are only covering the stories. So don't worry about the paperwork. Team D is going to manage all that. I will make sure all the paperwork is done on time. So don't worry! Focus on your story. Go and find something unique to present in front of the world. But also, make sure of your own safety! Okay? Now go! Time starts now!"

By saying that, the boss leaves the place.

"Guys, Boss is really upset this time! We have to make him proud. He's always been good to us, but... but the stories! We could not cover anything good within these three months. This is really shameful!" Employee 7 shares his opinion.

"Yes, guys, we really have to work hard this time," says Employee 3.

"Do any of you have some plans?" Employee 3 asks.

"I don't know, but we have to find something. Guys, let's think about it, do some research, and then from tomorrow onwards, we will start working on them separately according to team division." Employee 1 shares her opinion, and everybody seems happy with this idea.

"Okay, guys, let's go home."

"See you all tomorrow."

"Bye."

After that, all the employees went back to their homes and did some primary research on their own. The next morning, after reaching the office, all the employees announced their research.

"Guys! Did you find something unique?"

"Umm, nothing serious."

"I tried, but all the same, nothing to be filed as unique," explains all the employees one by one. Then suddenly, Employee 1 says, "Guys, I don't know, but I have found something. I am kind of confused about whether to cover it or not."

"What is it?"

"Actually, yesterday, after returning home, I was talking about the issue all the time. Then, while in the dining room, I listened to my kids talking about the new story that they heard from their school guard."

"Story from the school guard? You must be kidding us! How can you even think of covering that? There is no possibility," say other employees.

"No, no, not like that! It's not the way you think. It is something different." Cutting Employee 1's words, Employee 3 says, "Something different? How can it be different? It must be the same story for kings and queens. Or maybe a one-horned horse. Or the princess with a stepmother?"

"Aaa! Stop, please! Now listen to me," says Employee 1. The other employees said, "Yes, we are listening."

"It's about a train accident!"

"Train accident? Ummm...yes! Must be pathetic! But should we really cover it?"

"My kids are saying something miraculous happened back in that time."

"Miracle? What miracle? The train turned back to its initial position even after being crashed? Or all the people got back their lives even after death?"

"I don't know, but should we go to that school guard to know the entire story? To know what exactly happened."

"Okay! Let's give it a try! Team A, you guys work on it! Let's consider it your project!" Employee 8 advises this, and after that, all the employees confirm their approval.

"Let's go for it! Come on, Team A, go for your new project!" All of them started cheering for Team A. After that, Team A gathered all their necessary items and went in search of the school guard. They went to the school to find the school guard, but sadly, they could not find him. The school guard was on leave, and therefore, he went to his hometown for his holidays. Team A came back to the office with no fruit.

"Team A, how was your day? Did you find something to put on paper?" says the boss.

"Boss! You're here! I mean, how did you know?" Employee 2 asked as he was surprised.

"I am the boss! I must know what is going on in your mind." The boss laughs out loud and then asks, "Tell me what exactly happened. Day 1 has passed. Any updates on your project? Employee 1, could you find that school guard? What did he say? Something unique to start our work?" To clarify, employee 1 answers,

"Boss, we went in search of him, but we could not find him! He is on leave."

"Then what do you think? Should you end your research for this project right here? Or... um... what do you think, Employee 1?"

"No, boss! Day 1 has passed! I don't want to lose more time. I want to work on this project. Let's end what I have started," says employee 1.

"Very good! That's what I wanted to hear. I appreciate your courage, Employee 1! That's all I need. Now, tell me, what do you want to do next?"

"Boss, I guess I need a leave for one day. I want to go to the hometown of that school guard."

"Where is his hometown?"

"Darinda, Boss! It is a rural area."

"Well, quite an unknown place! You are not going alone. Employee 2, Employee 3, you are also going as a team. It's your teamwork now. How far is the place, Employee 1?" asks the boss.

"Not that far, actually! Three hours from here. If everything goes well, then we can cover it in one day."

"That's a good news, Team A! So, starting tomorrow morning, your journey begins. I am hoping for the best for you and be careful of everything that comes your way! Okay?"

"Yes, boss! We will take care of everything. Don't worry, boss, we are also hoping for the best," says Employee 1. After that, everyone cheered for Team A and wishes them good luck! The next day arrived, and in the early morning, Team A started their journey towards their mission, Darinda. After patiently waiting for three long hours, they reached their destination. The place was giving them the vibe of the old days. After reaching there, Team A starts looking for the school guard. It was not that hard for them to find the school guard, as he is one of those senior citizens who have lived for more than seven decades! After getting his address, Team A, without wasting any time, starts following the location. After some time, when Team A reaches there, they see a man working in his farm, wearing a loose shirt, loose trousers, and a hat on his head. He is farming in his late sixties! "Such a healthy and positive soul he is!" thought Employee 1 and allowed her to call out loud, "Sir, sir, here! This side! We are here in search of you." The man looked at them but didn't pay any attention.

"Umm, excuse me! Sir, sir, this side!" Team A keeps calling him repeatedly, but maybe he is not listening to them. To know what was going on, Employee 1, with her curious movement, went near him. "Excuse me, sir! We are here from a news channel. We are actually working on a project, so we need your help in that case."

"Yes! Who are you?"

The man's reaction left Employee 1 speechless. "Um, I mean, sir, for some time, we have been calling for you!"

"Calling me? Oh! I am so sorry, dear! Actually, I can't hear well, and something from a far distance is equal to impossible for me! I couldn't hear you, dear! I am extremely sorry for this behaviour!" explains the man. "Come this way." By doing so, the man led all the employees to his house. "I am old right now! The pain is getting more serious day by day and causing hearing problems. By the way, who are you, dear?"

"We are from a news channel. We are working on a project. So, we are here in search of you," says Employee 3. "Search for me?" The man turns back to the employee with a face full of doubt. "Why are you all in search of me, dear?"

"Actually, sir, my kids told me about the story that you told them while in school!" Employee 1 explains everything to the guard. "Oh! You came here from the school! But what is the story? I tell stories to all the kids literally every day. It makes me happy. Which story are you talking about?" Just after letting him finish his words, Employee 1 answers, "The story of the train accident! You told my kids that something miraculous happened at that time! What happened, sir? We are willing to know everything related to that. Please tell us! Share that incident with us, sir." The man looked at Employee 1 with disbelief. But after some time, that expression turned into a happy face. "Finally! Finally! Someone is talking about that incident after so many years. I knew it! We all knew it! She deserved much more! She deserved the entire universe! People should know about her! Yes! More people should know about her! She should be recalled and followed by the entire universe! You guys are going to write about her, right? Come and have a seat! I am going to tell you everything." Being confused because of the change of topic, Employee 1 asks the old man, "She? I mean, we were here to know about the train incident! But who is she? Without telling us about the accident, why are you telling us to know about her? I mean, that person!"

The old man replies with laughter and explains further, "That train accident would remain only an incident and had no more special reason to be focused if she was not there!"

"Who is she, sir?" The sudden urge to know the whole story jerks Employee 1.

"Alright, now listen carefully! It was the year 1984, and it was the rainy season. Our express train was running, loaded with many people. All the compartments were filled with different kinds of people from different places. There were different types of emotions lingering all over the air in different compartments. Different types of sounds were audible, like laughing men and women, playing kids, singing adults, duelling couples, and many more. I was one of them, returning from a family tour. In our compartment, there was a girl named Luna, a beautiful girl with a warm smile on her pretty face. Her vibe and behaviour were so clean that anyone could sense positivity and happiness around her! She talked to us, and we had good conversations over the journey. Her perspective on living a life was totally different from ours! She seemed to find happiness in the minimum things on this planet! Her happiness was too so pure as if the negativity couldn't dare to touch her vibe. She even played with our kids. Such a good girl she was! Everything was running smoothly, then all of a sudden, everything started shaking! Our lives and the entire train turned into a bloody hell within a minute. There was blood everywhere. The only visible thing there was the bloody, chopped flesh of human beings. The only audible sound there was the sound of painful crying and mourning. When I came back to my senses, I found myself covered with blood. My entire body was covered with several cuts and bruises. There was blood coming from my ears, and it was too painful! But you know, what was more painful than that? I found half of my family members lying dead next to me. Only my son was alive but left senseless! I tried many times. I truly tried many times to move, but my legs did not help me survive the situation. There was a huge pillar placed over my leg and blood was coming from my ear as my head was badly injured! In front of me, Luna was lying unconscious. From her stomach, blood was dripping continuously. All her beautiful, tender body was covered with cracked glasses! After some time, when the saviours came with an ambulance, people went crazy! They were wanting help, but surprisingly, they were only wanting help for themselves. After being rescued, nobody cared about others! There were too many people crying like lunatics for help, but they were not even noticed by others! Among all the affected people, there were many who were not that much injured. Despite some small cuts, they were all safe! But still, they didn't help others. They did not pay any attention to their fellow passengers. All of a sudden, a cruel side of humanity started to become visible everywhere! I was also one of them, crying for help. My kid was lying there unconscious, and I was begging for his help! A man who was one of my co-passengers was totally safe, but still, he did not even glance at my kid! I asked for help from him, but he, without any words, started to escape from that place. All he wanted was for his life to be safe, and he was completely fine! But there were tonnes of people lying and dying; it did not bother him, or every person like him.

Time passed, but no one came. The Saviour team was few in number, and there was a shortage of ambulances, so it was really time-consuming for them to help all the passengers of the train because there were so many affected people! I was all tired because of the unbearable pain in my legs, and my son was still lying unconscious! After some time, I could not help but close my eyes to take some rest from that pain. When I woke up, I saw Luna trying to get up from her condition. She tied a cloth around her stomach, which was also covered with blood, but she was trying to get up. I did not have any power in me to speak to her, but I was watching. I thought she was also one of them and would leave the place to save her life, but she did not. She did not! I was wrong! I was totally wrong! She did stand up, tied her stomach tightly, and without having any second thought, she picked my son up and ran somewhere. I could not say anything but stare at the empty door with a confused and suspicious look. For some reason, I suspected Luna! I still regret that! I suspected Luna! The pure soul, Luna! After some time, she came with some of the saviors. They saved me and brought me to the main camp. After reaching there, what I saw left me in shame! I found my son all safe and came back to his senses! Luna saved my son! I started crying; I misunderstood her! And you know what? After saving my son, she took the first-aid bag from the rescue team and went to help the other passengers. She was also in pain; blood was dripping continuously from her stomach. She was having a problem working, but still, she was working with all the saviours. Despite her horrible and painful situation, she was carrying a heavy bag containing many foods, water bottles, and a first aid kit. While someone was busy running towards their home, Luna kept working, except for being affected by the horrible accident. The entire day passed, but still, she kept working with the Saviour team. Though I was not present there, I left for the hospital. I went through surgery and was unconscious for a long period of time. But when I woke up, I heard the saddest news ever, and I was not prepared for that! Luna was no more. Due to the unbearable pain, she lost her life while working on the platform to save others. But do you know what was most heart-breaking? That girl was dying, and there was nothing left in her, but what she did left all the people present there devoted to her. She declared the donation of her safe body organs to those who were in need of them while being affected by the accident. She also shared all of her bank details with the saviours because she wanted all of her money to be donated to all of the affected people." By saying that, the old man got up from his seat. "Come on! There is something I want to show you," he starts walking towards somewhere, and the speechless us keep following him. Within some steps, we reach behind the train station. It is a beautiful garden field with beautiful, colourful flowers. "What is this place, sir?" asks Employee 1.

"It was established in memory of Beatrix."

"Who is Beatrix now, sir?"

"Because of Luna's incomparable courage and positive thinking, the people back in that day bestowed on her the title of BEATRIX! They all established this place as a memory of the brave and kind Beatrix. And here lies the queen of the garden!" The old man points his gesture towards a tombstone. The tombstone is shining with its own positive vibe! It is covered with numerous beautiful flowers, and the name on the nameplate has a different positive vibe.

BEATRIX

Luna Hope (1963–1984)

The big font of the title is sharing a new message with us. "When Beatrix died, she wore a beautiful white gown, and she was covered with numerous pretty flowers. She was looking like a queen that day! And her face was glowing and shining with an elegant smile. After that day, all the visitors kept planting many flowering plants in this field, and from that day, I have been taking care of this garden. It is a beautiful garden with many beautiful souls. The positive thinking of Beatrix was an inspiration to many souls! But don't worry, this garden is holy, and we are trying our best to protect this pure place from the evil powers! Though there were many people who became jealous because of Beatrix's good work, they are obviously dead souls. The delightful kindness of Beatrix was a toxin to their negativity! Those poor souls! I always feel pity for them. People say, there are still some bad spirits roaming around this place to get in touch with Beatrix, in order to be free! Beatrix gave a new purpose to my life! I feel so proud that I got to spend some time with her in my lifetime. To witness such kindness in this cruel world is such a miracle to me." The old man ends his story, leaving Team A crying with extreme happiness. Employee 1 picks up her phone and dials the number of their boss. "Yes, Employee 1, what is going on there? Any updates on your project? Could you find anything?" Employee 1 answers with a smile of satisfaction on her face. "Yes, sir! I have just found a new inspiration to frame in front of the entire world. What could be more unique than finding a miracle in this cruel practical world?" After a few days, suddenly one morning, to give lessons to the youth and the old, a separate paragraph is shining brightly on the front page of a weekly newspaper, titled 'A NEW HOPE'.

Epilogue

Approximately two and a half years ago, I was travelling by train. When the train stopped at a particular platform for almost 15 minutes, I noticed a common behaviour among all the people on that platform. They were all somehow busy! Very busy to even look at their surroundings to see if anyone was in need of help or not! Their activities were more like if they were about to catch their last train of life or something. All the anxious faces were making me feel weird! And there were some other people who were either roaming around or sitting in a corner of that platform with no hope left within them. Some of them were trying to give it another shot by asking for help, but it couldn't help them as their existence was nothing to those busy people. The difference between two genres of people was disturbing me to hell. The entire view was more like a haunted place to me, as if I were witnessing ghosts everywhere. There were two types of ghosts: one who became dead out of no hope in life, and on the other hand, one who became dead out of no emotion and no life within them. As an artist, I observed every detail of that platform very carefully and thought to draw it later on canvas. But after returning home, I couldn't do that. That situation shattered me and even my artistic self! So as a result, I had to put down my brush and failed to make art. After some months of that incident, somehow, I started working for humanity. Things kept changing for me as I was helping lives as much as possible. From humans to animals, I try to do as much as I can. But while working on that selfless purpose, I tend to be disturbed by the behaviour of other people! Sometimes they are preventing me from doing a good job, and sometimes they are praising me as a hero or something for doing the same good job. But while praising, they always forget they can be the hero too, instead of just being a regular viewer! Instead of saying the same phrase, "We need more people like you," they can become the Person Like Me by themselves! It's actually not that hard to become a hero, and now that I have the chance to publish my first book, I can finally convert my feelings into an artistic form. Beatrix was just a regular girl; her actions and her empathy made her the hero. It's not like she was born with some superpower or that kind of stuff! Personally, what I feel is that everyone has a superpower within them; it's just a choice to generate the superpower into reality or just keep living like a dead soul. Not only on platforms, but everywhere people also pretend to be busy and ignore those who are dying out of no care and attention, as if it's their destiny. But why don't they think they can change destiny too if they can change their perspective first? Cruelty towards animals, nature, and even humans is rising continuously. We have to make a choice right now. Choice: to be a dead soul or to be a real human being.

While working for humanity, I often got to hear the word "mad" from others. Others who can't tolerate bad work but keep protesting against good work simultaneously! I don't have much to say to those dead souls, but I have many to suggest to my readers, so I wrote 'Station of Dead Hearts'. If any of you liked the character Beatrix and got the courage to be the real-life Beatrix, then the only person who would be very happy is the 'Mad' me! It's nothing but a choice to generate the courage to take the first step into reality. There's a sentence that always prompts and encourages me to do something good—'If not me, then who!' It's just about a single step to take, dear readers! I just want you to think the same and be the next Beatrix. After all, being mad is not an easy joke; only legends can do that! LOL! The example of a platform is just a small perspective. If we can start from that, then there will be a day when everyone will be enlightened by the true meaning of humanity. Always remember that someone, somewhere is waiting for you to help them, and you can make the miracle happen by just taking the first step. Thank you so much for coming this far and reading the entire book. As it is my first book, so I'm asking your pardon and understanding at the same time, for all the mistakes that I have made while writing this book. I hope you will only consume positive among all the negativity around. I wish you a happy and fulfilling life ahead. I sincerely believe in Beatrix and her story. I hope you do, too.

Acknowledgements

If the story of Beatrix has inspired any of my readers, then I am thankful to them!

I am thankful for all the positive energy in the entire universe that keeps me motivated to take the initiative to do all the good work.

I'm thankful to all the elements of Mother Nature for helping me find the inner peace within me.

I'm thankful to Ruskin Bond, sir, whose books and writings inspired me to be a writer.

I'm thankful to my beloved (MY), without him and his eternal support, Falguni Ephji is incomplete.

I'm thankful to Tofu and the late RupKotha, who were always there when I felt like giving up.

I'm thankful to my parents for helping me manage my mundane life.

I'm thankful to all those people in my surroundings who kept trying to pull me down with their zero intelligence and virtue; without their negativity, I would never be able to stand stronger with my positivity.

I'm thankful to me for keeping believing in myself, and I'm very much thankful for my anger issue, because without that, I'm nothing.

My special thanks and regards to all of those positive, courageous, and mad souls who continuously work as an antidote to all the dead souls on the planet. Their existence makes me feel proud to be a human every day. I honestly don't believe in God or demons, but I do believe in them and their good works! I wish them a happy and healthy life ahead.

The entire story is based on the law of Karma and how it works. I'm thankful to the only idol of my life, Shani Dev (the *Karmafal* Data according to Hindu mythology). I'm living my life on the right path just because of him and our love, so I'm thankful to the entire universe for gifting me my DEV. I believe in KARMA, and I want everyone to believe in that too.

FALGUNI EPHJI is a creative soul who believes in the beauty of art and appreciates it in its every form. Life is also an art, according to her, and as a believer in its beauty, she prefers humanity over any other materialistic things. She believes it is important to take the first step to make a change! From her empathetic view of humanity, she wrote her first novella, 'Station of Dead Hearts'. This book was written to encourage every positive soul to take the brave initiative to do something for the better future of humanity.

An artwork titled 'A New Hope'
by Falguni Ephji created to describe this story.

We love creating beautiful books for you!

Be a part of our ever-growing community of authors.
Grow, write, and publish with us!

Connect with us on socials.
We'd love to hear from you!

@InkfeathersPublishing

www.ingramcontent.com/pod-product-compliance
Lightning Source LLC
LaVergne TN
LVHW041127150826
845673LV00007B/2210